POSITIVELY
TOTALLY
JTT!

He's the hottest new teen star on the big and small screens, but a full schedule, millions of fans, and countless charitable appearances haven't stopped Jonathan Taylor Thomas from adding more projects to his full plate! They're all here, from his hit TV show, *Home Improvement,* to blockbuster movies like Disney's *The Lion King, Man of the House, Tom and Huck* and *Pinocchio.*

Join him behind the scenes and learn what's it's like to work with Tim Allen, Chevy Chase, Farrah Fawcett and others; the perks and pitfalls of stardom; how he makes time for his favorite causes; what kind of girl appeals to him—and more!

Read all about the guy you'd love to meet ...

Jonathan Taylor Thomas!

Jonathan Taylor Thomas

TOTALLY

JTT!

An Unauthorized Biography

Michael-Anne Johns

AN ARCHWAY PAPERBACK
Published by POCKET BOOKS
New York London Toronto Sydney Tokyo Singapore

AN ARCHWAY PAPERBACK *Original*

An Archway Paperback published by
POCKET BOOKS, a division of Simon & Schuster Inc.
1230 Avenue of the Americas, New York, NY 10020

ISBN: 0-671-56272-X

First Archway Paperback printing January 1996

10 9 8 7 6 5 4 3 2 1

AN ARCHWAY PAPERBACK and colophon are registered trademarks of Simon & Schuster Inc.

Cover photos by Christopher Voelker / Shooting Star

Printed in the U.S.A.

IL 5+

To the *real* teen angel—thank you.

CONTENTS

INTRODUCTION

Jonathan Taylor Thomas—he's the #1 Teen Star on the #1 TV show, *Home Improvement,* and in the #1 movie of all time, *The Lion King!*

With all these credits—and lots more—to his name, it's amazing to realize JTT is only fourteen years old! And he hasn't even scratched the surface of his talent yet. But there's a lot more to this raspy-voiced cutey who has garnered millions of fans via his TV and movie work. He isn't the most popular teen star all over the world *just* because he's cute and funny. No, there's much, much more to JTT, and within these pages you'll get to know what makes him so special.

You can't pass a newsstand without seeing JTT's smiling face on all the covers of the teen magazines. But when you open those fan mags, you get just a taste of the real dynamo who has taken Hollywood by storm. Now you can find out the full story: where he came from; how he got started in show business; what he's like at home and on the set of *Home Improvement;* who he's friends with; his upcoming projects; and what is really near and dear to his heart.

What many may find surprising is that, in spite of his young age, JTT has reached out and touched more than fans, more than TV and movie viewers. Influenced by his mom, Claudine, who was once a social worker, JTT has a desire to help those who need it the most. Involved with many organized charities, he understands that a little of his time can make the day for children who aren't as fortunate as he. Whether it's visiting kids in hospitals or working on a telethon to encourage kids to pledge community service, JTT is there. It's a fact, he will do anything he can to make other kids happy.

But there's even more here. There's the behind-the-scenes rumors that circulate about any star—and the truth about all of them! There's a peep at what life is like on the set of *Home Improvement*—and the laugh-a-minute relationship he has with his TV dad, Tim Allen. There's the heartwarming relationship JTT has with his mom and his older brother, Joel. And there's the answer to the question: Why is JTT so popular?

JTT isn't your typical shooting star. He's *different,* and that quality is going to keep him front and center for a long time to come. The fact is, the only thing he really shares with his smart-alecky TV character, Randy, is his unfailing energy. In reality, JTT is one of the *most* compassionate, spirited, articulate, highly intelligent kids you would want to meet. And his fans recognize this. That's why he truly inspires them. He demands the best in himself, and he brings out the best in others.

Enjoy this very private look at JTT, and you'll find out to *know* him to is to definitely *love* him!

Jonathan Taylor Thomas

TOTALLY
JTT!

BABY STEPS

B-u-z-z-z-z!! The sound of the alarm clock is a familiar one to Jonathan Taylor Thomas. It goes off every
weekday morning exactly at 7:00 A.M., but Jonathan
rarely needs it to rouse him. By the time it rings,
he's usually been stirring for at least a half hour,
tossing in bed, considering the day ahead. Like most
of his days, this will be a busy one. He listens for
the footsteps coming up the stairs toward his room.
Momentarily, his mom will knock on the door and
poke her head in, "just checking" to make sure he's
on schedule. She always does that. Claudine Thomas
has been up for hours and fixed breakfast for her
two sons.

Jonathan bumps into his older brother, Joel, who
has dressed, eaten breakfast, and even walked the
dog by this early hour. Joel, who's in high school,
has to be there at 7:30, while Jonathan has the luxury
of another half hour before his day really begins. He

trundles off to the shower, humming a tune he heard on the radio the night before.

To an outsider looking in, the scene seems ordinary enough: a typical American family getting ready to start the day. But appearances can sometimes be deceiving. In fact, there's little that's "ordinary" about Jonathan Taylor Thomas and his life. Extraordinary is more like it. Extraordinary is what *he* has always been.

Jonathan was born in Bethlehem, a small city in eastern Pennsylvania, bordered by the Lehigh River, north of Philadelphia. While the name may suggest some link to the identically named biblical town in Israel, this city bears little resemblance to the historical one near Jerusalem. This Bethlehem is known less for its religious significance than for its industrial significance. It has always been a major steel-producing center, and the smokestacks from the steel mills cast a gray pallor over the city that make it look depressed, even when the economy is healthy.

The major employer in town is Bethlehem Steel. Many people who live in the area work for that company. Jonathan's dad, Stephen, whose family has longtime roots in that area, was an industrial sales manager there. His wife, Claudine, was a social worker. By the time they welcomed their second child into their home, on September 8, 1981, they were already parents to three-and-a-half-year-old Joel. Stephen and Claudine named Joel's baby brother Jonathan. That is what they have always called him, never Jon, and certainly not Johnny. His nickname, JTT, wasn't given to him by his family but by the millions of adoring fans he'd have somewhat later on. That's getting ahead of our story, although even as an infant, Jonathan had his share of admirers.

All babies are beautiful, but baby Jonathan was something else again. He had fine, white-blond hair and bright blue eyes. His dimpled smile seemed permanently affixed. As a tiny tot, Jonathan lit up a room the moment he crawled into it.

They say that second children are by nature outgoing because they are born into a "social" situation—there's already another child in the house they have to interact with. That may not be the case every time, but it certainly was by nature, and by nurture, with Jonathan, whose natural inclination was one of friendship and acceptance of others. He wasn't the kind of kid who hid behind his mom's skirts when a newcomer approached but one who was eager to be in on the conversation.

Precocious and curious, Jonathan was an early talker, quick on the pickup, artfully mimicking everything he heard. Always good-natured, he was extraordinarily alert, observant, and happy. In many ways, Jonathan seemed a step ahead of his pint-size peers. He was the kind of toddler so obviously different and special that people would stop his parents in the street to admire him. Jonathan doesn't really remember his earliest years, but his mom does. As Claudine recently noted, "At eighteen months old, Jonathan seemed older than his age, and he was really outgo-

3

ing. Everyone kept saying, 'Wow! Why don't you put him on television?' "

They might as well have been saying "Why don't you send him to the moon?" For showbiz was not part of their world. No one they knew had the slightest interest or inclination about performing professionally. To them, showbiz was just that fantasy world found on the other side of a movie or TV screen. By and large, folks in Bethlehem were hard-working everyday people who were entertained by actors—they didn't become actors themselves.

There was another reason Jonathan's family scoffed at the showbiz suggestions of their neighbors. It's one that has been so deeply ingrained in Jonathan from his earliest years that it still infuses everything he does today. Jonathan has always been taught to look outside himself—not inside—for satisfaction. He has always heard that putting others first was more important and, in the end, more rewarding than "looking out for number one." Seeing how you could lend a hand to your neighbor, school, and community is what counted. That's what made you special and worthwhile, and that's what brought joy and fulfillment.

It wasn't just some idealistic sentiment, for the concept of helping others was practiced every day in Jonathan's household. His mom trained as a social worker, and for the first impressionable years of Jonathan's life, she worked with handicapped and mentally disabled people. Sometimes she brought her own kids to work with her. Being around people who were physically and mentally challenged made a lasting impression on such a bright, observant youngster as Jonathan. He has never forgotten what he saw. When asked today about those early experiences, Jonathan explains, "My mom just brought me up to care about others," as if it were the most natural thing in the world. To him, it was.

Still, others continued to exclaim about how cute and animated he was, how he should really be on TV. That really registered with Jonathan. For little JTT actually understood what people were talking about. Although his parents weren't picking up on it, Jonathan didn't just forget. He just kept it in the back of his fertile, growing young mind.

Around the tender age of four, Jonathan made two significant decisions. They didn't necessarily relate to each other, but interestingly enough, he hasn't wavered from either of them yet. He remembers them quite clearly. One led him to become a vegetarian. "When I was four, I ate a lot of meat products," he explained, "but after that year, I just started editing out and dropping things from my diet—I'll eventually get to where I'm a total vegetarian." Jonathan may not have been completely clear about why he made those changes. It just seemed right and natural to him.

The other decision also seemed right and natural. It would be several more years until he was able to actually do what he determined to, though: at the age of four, Jonathan declared that yes, he was going to be on TV someday.

A MODEL CHILD

When Jonathan was four and a half, he and his family moved to a suburb of Sacramento, California, where his dad had gotten a new job as an industrial sales manager. Situated in the northern part of the state, Sacramento is about ninety miles northeast of San Francisco; nearly four hundred miles away from Los Angeles. While those statistics meant nothing to Jonathan at the time; they would become very significant in the not-too-distant future.

Picking up and moving an entire family is never easy, but Jonathan's clan actually looked forward to making new friends and putting down roots in this clean, growing city. In 1986, when Jonathan's family moved there, many of the surrounding suburbs of Sacramento were new and filled with young families. Houses were spacious with wide lawns. Driveways, more often than not, were dotted with basketball hoops and two-wheelers. The neighborhoods seemed pristine compared with Bethlehem; just perfect for bringing up two young boys. The school system was well regarded and most parents were quite active and involved in the education of their children. Jonathan and his attentive, well-educated, involved parents fit in perfectly; and before long, the family had settled in. Stephen and Claudine—who continued in social work—were in their new jobs; Joel and Jonathan adapted quickly to their new lives and schools.

Both boys were extremely active and had natural grace and athletic ability. Soccer was one of the first organized sports they played. Jonathan, who remembers sitting on the sidelines watching his big brother play, got his chance when he was just five years old to join a team in a neighborhood kiddie league. Speedy, focused, and competitive, Jonathan was a natural from the get-go. Once he learned the rules, he could play either offense or defense with equal agility. He was quickly recognized as one of the team's star players, but Jonathan wasn't a show-off. Generous on the field, outgoing, and chatty, he made many friends on his team.

Soccer became a big part of his young life. Aside from learning the basics of a sport that would stay with him, Jonathan also learned something else of value. He got experience in taking direction, following the instructions of a coach or manager. It was a skill that would come in handy in situations far from a soccer field.

In Sacramento, Jonathan took up another pursuit that brought him a lot of pleasure—fishing. He used to go on weekends with his brother and dad to the nearby lakes that ringed the city. He learned to love the peaceful solitude of sitting on a boat out on the lake and then feeling the excitement of a tug on the line. Fishing became his favorite thing to do on vacation, and over the next several years, he was lucky enough to fish in such exotic places as Mexico, Hawaii, and even off the coast of Alaska. "That's where I caught the greatest salmon and halibut," he remembers. He was so interested in the sport that he even began subscribing to publications devoted to it. "I've been reading fishing magazines since I was five," he recently noted. That was no exaggeration: Jonathan started reading at four.

When he turned six, Jonathan followed his brother into elementary school. No surprise, JTT adapted to that as easily as he had to his new home, neighborhood, and soccer pals. His giftedness was recognized early. He was very advanced in reading, writing, and arithmetic. Once he was taught something, he remembered it. He was immediately placed in an advanced reading group and flew through elementary arithmetic; in first grade, he'd quickly mastered addition and subtraction and was doing third-grade multiplication.

But Jonathan's gifts were not limited to academics. In a way, he was just as gifted socially. Extremely bright and exuberant, little Jonathan was accepted immediately by his new peers and his teachers. There is one memorable incident that really illustrates the kind of kid Jonathan was—and still is.

Each week one child was chosen as "student of the week" and, among other tasks, asked to make a list of six friends. The week Jonathan was chosen, he did something no other kid in that class ever did before, and no one has done since. He stood up and explained to the class that just because he was listing six of them didn't mean he was excluding the others. He went on to say he was still friends with all of them. That sensitivity and kindness is pure Jonathan Taylor Thomas—then, and even more so, now.

Jonathan had successfully settled in to his new life in Sacramento—he was living a busy normal little boy's life at home, at school, and on the soccer field. But this little boy never did forget the idea planted in his brain when he was smaller. He never forgot those people who kept telling his parents that he really ought to be in showbiz. He certainly never forgot about his own decision to be on TV one day. "I just thought the whole idea of being on TV and being recognized and having a good time was interesting, pretty cool" is how he simply remembers it.

Then one day when he was six, Jonathan saw an advertisement on TV that piqued that interest. Aimed at young children and their parents, the commercial said that if you signed up for a thirteen-week course, you could learn how to get into commercials. It was all Jonathan needed to hear. He was off and bugging—his mom, that is, to let him take that course. After some time had gone by and some investigating to make sure the place was not a rip-off, Claudine agreed that it would be okay for Jonathan to sign up. He has never regretted that day.

Although the course itself didn't immediately propel its students into national television commercials,

Jonathan and the others enrolled did learn how to model clothes for catalogs, to pose for department store fashion shows, and to project confidence and charisma. Of the last two, Jonathan didn't have much to learn: he was naturally confident, cute, and charismatic. After the thirteen weeks, the school sponsored a graduation dinner where the students modeled clothes and demonstrated the poise they'd learned. Of course, family and friends attended, but to the school's credit, so did a few talent scouts. If these scouts weren't exactly from Hollywood (and they weren't), some were from as far away as San Francisco, a media center in its own right. No surprise, Jonathan was snapped up immediately by a talent scout from a San Francisco agency called Grimme Talent.

It took some persuasion for Claudine to allow Jonathan, who was barely seven years old at the time, to sign up. Had she known what would follow—two-hour drives each way back and forth from Sacramento to San Francisco, just so Jonathan could try out for modeling assignments!—she might have thought twice before agreeing. For once committed to something, Claudine was not the type to do it halfway or halfheartedly. If she allowed Jonathan to do this, she would support him wholly and try to make his new endeavor disrupt the other members of the family as little as possible. It is to her credit that she did—and to Jonathan's that he learned valuable lessons in dedication and commitment by her example.

Besides, Claudine could see how enthusiastic Jonathan was. Anyone could see how perfect he was—it didn't take a crystal ball to predict just how successful he'd eventually be.

Under the guidance of Anne Grimme, owner of the agency, Jonathan appeared in fashion shows and started to model clothing in kids' catalogs for San Francisco department stores. He also appeared in magazine and newspaper advertisements. Sometimes the modeling would mean he'd have to miss a day or two of first or second grade, but he never blew off any of his schoolwork. Jonathan always knew to put schoolwork first. Not only did he always make up assignments, he began a practice that he adheres to today: doing more work than is required. Call him an "extra-credit" kid.

More to his personal "extra credit," Jonathan never bragged about his burgeoning modeling career. While another kid might reenter the classroom with an even bigger ego after coming out in a big fashion spread, Jonathan took pains to show and tell what he was doing, not show off and tell. He once brought in some of the clothes he was modeling, along with some black-and-white proofs, and explained to the class about the process of creating an advertisement. Bringing others into his world, without bragging about it, has always made Jonathan happier than any individual achievement.

His world, however, was getting busier by the nanosecond. It didn't take long for Jonathan to progress from standing still and silent in advertisements to being animated and articulate on stage. Jonathan first displayed his natural acting ability in a local production of the play *Scrooge* at the Chatauqua Theater in Sacramento—in a dual role, no less. He played both the parts of young Scrooge and Tiny Tim in a holiday production and received glowing reviews and standing ovations. He also developed an affinity for acting. The kind of acting he would do, and everything it would lead to, would make his life much more complicated, but he has never lost that love for the craft itself.

In the earliest stages of his career, Jonathan also began doing something that would ultimately lead to his big break. Voice-overs is the show business industry term for any type of narration: any situation where the actor's voice is heard, but he or she is not seen. That includes all radio work, most commercials, many TV shows and movies, including all animated films.

Jonathan modestly describes his speaking voice as "just an ordinary kid's voice," but anyone who has ever heard him knows just how distinct that voice is. As opposed to the high-pitched, squeaky tone most young children have, Jonathan's is raspy and gravelly. It's an all-boy voice, curious, mischievous, distinctly discernible. That recognizability combined with Jonathan's superior reading skills, ability to take direction, and natural acting talent made him perfect for voice-over work—and lots of it came his way.

The first voice-over commercial he ever did was a true test of his talent—it was in Japanese! To the animated actions of a character speaking in Japanese, Jonathan had to speak the words in English, make it convincing, and sound right. He executed it perfectly. It was a great experience for all that was soon to come.

It had been a year since he took that thirteen-week course. Jonathan was incredibly successful, and each step led to the next. Perhaps that next step might not have come quite so quickly if Jonathan and his mom hadn't attended a seminar given by a Hollywood talent manager, but they did. And if that day didn't change the course of Jonathan's life, it sure speeded it up.

The seminar was mainly for parents who wanted to learn about children and show business: how to get in, and what to expect if you got there. Given in various parts of the country by a respected manager, it taught parents with no connections what type of child was likely to be successful as an actor, and which would have a harder time getting started. Normally, a certain precociousness is valued. While a timid child would find it tough breaking in, a child who speaks easily and articulately, who can interpret the words on a page and perform them (not just read them), who can take direction, given by a stranger— and who, for good measure, is adorable—would not only attract the attention of an agent but would probably find work easily and often. Naturally, those traits described Jonathan right down to his button nose and ever ready smile. At the end of the seminar, those who were still interested were invited for an impromptu audition. Jonathan was interested.

Gary Scalzo was the Hollywood manager and he knew talent when he found it. He was the man responsible for bringing Elijah Wood (*The Good Son,*

North, The War) from the cornfields of Iowa to the movie screens of Hollywood; he discovered *Step by Step*'s Angela Watson and *The Brady Bunch*'s Paul Sutera, who both attended seminars in Florida. Gary was soon to convince Jonathan and his mother that Hollywood was waiting—and he could help.

Gary had a system set up, where he brought his most promising finds to Hollywood, got them set up in an apartment complex, and hooked them up with legitimate agents. The agents would then send the kids out on auditions for commercials, TV shows, and even movies.

Not very many people who attended Gary's seminars actually made the move to Hollywood. After all, it takes an incredible dedication to uproot a family and relocate—even if it's just for a few months to test the showbiz waters. How many parents, after all, can quit (or take leaves of absence from) their jobs, and leave spouses and other children in the family behind to pursue what amounts to a dream—an uncertain one at that. The reality is that most people—children and adults—who want to become actors never do. They may try out hundreds of times, but they don't land the parts. If they do, the parts aren't numerous or lucrative enough to pay the bills.

And there is that—the expense—to consider, too. For although Gary was committed to helping these talented tykes break into showbiz, the families footed the bills: for transportation, rent, food, clothing to go to auditions in, all living expenses. And most, of course, maintained households in whatever other part of the country they came from. Showbiz might eventually be glamorous and financially rewarding, but it almost never starts out that way.

It takes an extraordinary and dedicated family to make all these sacrifices. But Jonathan, an extrordinary child, was lucky enough to have one. He was intrigued by Gary's suggestion. After all, he'd gotten a taste of acting and knew he wanted to do more.

After much careful thought and consideration, Claudine agreed to give it a try. She and Jonathan made the four-hundred-mile drive down to Los Angeles just to see if they could really do this. If several months passed and Jonathan didn't land an acting job or was unhappy, they'd simply go back home. Of course, it never came to that. Not only was Jonathan successful from the start, he clearly loved every second of what would soon be his new life.

Mother and son settled into an apartment complex where several of Gary's other finds—Angela Watson and her mom; Paul Sutera and his; Carol Ann Plante (who eventually landed a role on the syndicated TV series *Harry and the Hendersons*) and her mom— were doing the same thing, "testing the waters" to see if their talented children could break into show-biz and, more importantly, be happy and live a normal life, too.

They all have particularly wonderful memories of the little community formed by these people from different parts of the country, joined together by Gary Scalzo and a common dream. Paul Sutera, Elijah Wood, Carol Ann Plante, Angie Watson and Jonathan were all there to support one another. No one was jealous. If one of the kids had an audition and needed something to wear to it, the others would run to their closets to see if they had something to lend. And the kids would practice their scripts together, read monologues, and help each other memorize them.

The best part was when the little group of actor hopefuls got together and put on impromptu plays. Once the group put on *The Wizard of Oz*. They made their own costumes and performed this little play for each other. To the parents watching them perform it was a reaffirmation of why they were there in the first place. They really *were* little actors.

Gary Scalzo, of course, kept a steady hand in the progress of his group and delivered what he'd promised: to help each one sign up with an agent and coach them for auditions.

The agency Jonathan signed with was called Helfond, Joseph and Rix. It had a particularly successful and active children's department at the time. His new agent saw Jonathan's potential immediately. Jonathan was the kind of kid casting directors clamor for: he could read and memorize scripts easily and all those years playing soccer had taught him to take direction well. Plus, Jonathan had another quality that could not be taught. He simply sparkled when he walked into a room—even a roomful of strangers for whom he had to perform. Everyone remembered him.

The sparkle was no act. Jonathan truly loved being in Los Angeles among this little group of talented peers. He even enjoyed auditions, which most actors dread. He wasn't upset if he didn't get the role he was up for; he simply prepared for the next one. He thrived on all of it. Seeing new places, meeting new people, and facing a new challenge each day didn't frighten Jonathan. He saw it as a whole new world, the one in which he truly belonged.

Within two weeks of arriving in Los Angeles he landed his first national commercial! In at least one way it really tested Jonathan's acting ability. The commercial was for the giant fast-food chain Burger King, and by that time, Jonathan, a vegetarian, hadn't eaten red meat in three years. Yet the budding professional did a more than convincing job of making the burgers look appetizing.

Within another few weeks, the tiny thespian tried out and was hired for several more television commercials. He appeared in regional ads for such products as Kern's bread and Vivident gum, and in national ads for Kellogg's Product 19, Mattel Toys, and Canon Camcorders. Jonathan also nabbed a role in an industrial film. It wasn't shown to the public, but he did get his first on-camera experience, as well as entry into the Screen Actor's Guild, the organization all working actors must join.

It was when he signed up for SAG that he found he couldn't use his birth name professionally. There already was an actor registered by that name and the rules state that no two actors can go under the identical name. That's when he became, for professional purposes, Jonathan Taylor Thomas. Taylor was his own middle name; Thomas was Joel's.

Racking up acting credits and on-screen experience was on-the-job training for Jonathan. Never during his early days in Los Angeles did anyone suggest acting lessons. Jonathan's timing, his emoting, his comic ability, all came naturally. It was just his gift.

At this point, even though Jonathan was landing commercials one after the other, he and his mom still weren't sure how much longer they could stay in Los Angeles. As successful as he was in commercials, they questioned whether that was enough to pull up stakes and relocate permanently. As it was, whenever Jonathan was between auditions and commercials, he and his mom journeyed back to Sacramento to resume their "normal" lives. Jonathan would rejoin his class, picking up as if he'd never left, only to depart again when another acting opportunity came along. Being flexible has served him well.

In early 1990 Jonathan got the opportunity to try out for his first television series. *The Bradys* was a half-hour CBS sitcom revolving around the lives of the now grown-up Brady bunch. The actors who'd played the kids on that legendary '70s series were all reprising their roles, this time as adults with their own families. Barry Williams, who played Greg, the oldest of the original bunch, would be married and a dad in *The Bradys*. The part of his son Kevin went to Jonathan.

Playing Kevin was a neat piece of acting on Jonathan's part. For the character was completely unlike him in real life. Kevin was the scriptwriter's idea of a seven-year-old—not very articulate, extremely silly, and childish. Jonathan, of course, was never like that;

but when he stepped into Kevin's sneakers, he became the character completely.

Being on a television series changed everything for Jonathan and his mom. It was a whole new schedule, a whole new lifestyle: and JTT, as usual, was a quick picker-upper of the ropes. Even though he didn't work every day on the show—because of the large ensemble cast, no one really had to—he was required to be in Los Angeles and be available on a moment's notice. The studio provided a tutor who would get assignments from his third-grade teacher in Sacramento. He found out that kids on TV shows were required to put in only three hours of schooling per day. From day one, Jonathan always put in more.

Being on *The Bradys* was his first experience with the lifestyle of a young TV actor. And Jonathan liked it an awful lot. He had no trouble adapting to his new schedule—being on the set one day, working with a tutor and actor, being home the next, and so on.

He reveled in the challenge of playing a kid so very different from himself. He got along well with all the adults in the cast and became friends with all the kids. In between scenes, he and the other kids in the cast would go outside on the Paramount Studios lot, where *The Bradys* was taped, to play. Sometimes they'd run around playing tag, other times they'd toss a football around.

One memorable day JTT was playing ball with Michael Melby, who played Mickey Logan on *The Bradys*, when who should walk over to them but comedian Arsenio Hall. At the time Arsenio was hosting his own very popular late-night show, which just happened to tape over at Paramount. A sports lover himself, he took a few moments to hang out with Jonathan and his little buddy. The next day Arsenio came back to where the kids were playing—this time, bearing a gift. It was an autographed Nerf football for Jonathan.

Naturally, JTT, all of nine years old at the time, was thrilled. Arsenio was a big star, and here was an autographed treasure. Not surprisingly, his elation was not shared by the other little actor. "He was kind of upset that Arsenio had given the ball to me and not to him," Jonathan remembers. Without a moment's hesitation—and without any prompting from anyone—Jonathan simply gave his treasure to his young costar. It was a typical move for big-hearted Jonathan, who couldn't bear to see someone left out. He still can't.

Jonathan's largesse didn't go completely unrewarded. His mom, who all along had been the one to teach him respect for the feelings of others, went out and bought him a similar Nerf football. Of course, it had no autograph, so it wasn't the same, but it did symbolize just how nice Jonathan had been. That football remains on a shelf in his room to this day.

The Bradys, which began its run on CBS in September 1990, was Jonathan's true first taste of being a regular on a TV series. It tasted good. Jonathan learned by leaps and bounds—how to work with an ensemble cast, how to take direction, hit his marks, memorize his script and deliver his lines, and create a believable character.

He learned something else about life in the show-biz lane—all about disappointment. For just as JTT was getting used to his new routine, *The Bradys* was abruptly canceled after seven airings! It hadn't done well in the ratings, and the network simply exercised its option to cease production. No further explanation was required: the sets were torn down and the actors told not to report to work anymore.

Suddenly Jonathan was jobless. He knew he and the other actors had done really good work, but he found out that in showbiz being good at what you do isn't always enough. He began to understand the role *luck*—and timing—play in this world.

Although he didn't know it at the time, an improvement in his luck was just around the corner.

A NEW *HOME*

There's an old saying, "When one door closes, another opens." The message is to not let disappointment get you down, because another opportunity is often right around the corner. In Jonathan's case, everything happened so quickly, that adage could have been about a revolving door. Before he could shed too many tears about the *Bradys* bust-up, a new opportunity presented itself. It was early 1991, and he was sent by his agent on an audition for a new TV series. The part JTT was up for was the middle child in a family comedy called (at that early stage of its development and predating the famous rap song) *Hammer Time.*

On the surface, *Hammer Time* was a comedy version of *This Old House*—about a real "Mr. Fix-It" type named Tim Taylor who relies on what's in his tool belt, instead of what's in his head, to solve life's everyday problems. Tim is a married dad of three and host of a cable TV show that demonstrates the "do-it-yourself" method of building and repairing things around the house. Tim's also a bit of a chauvinist who prides himself on his "ultra manly" attitude. It doesn't work on the cable show, where it's obvious that his assistant, Al, is really the one with the know-how, and it certainly doesn't work at home, where his wife, Jill, rules the roost.

Still, armed with his hefty tool belt and an endless variety of power tools, Tim believes himself the master of every household problem from leaky faucets to sticky cabinets. The bigger problem is that he approaches every project as an opportunity to reaffirm his masculinity—usually at the expense of whatever he's ostensibly fixing. The dishwasher broken? "Let's rewire it to give it more power!" is a typical Tim solution. Of course, the "fixed" appliance blows up afterward.

Just below the surface—not too far, really—*Hammer Time* was really about the differences between the way men and women approach life. While spunky Jill Taylor is completely devoted to Tim, she understands her hardware-hungry husband all too well—at least enough not to let him near any household appliances. As the mother of three rambunctious sons, Jill knows plenty about handling mischievous boys of any age. Jill was the real power *chez* Taylor, the engine that drives the household (and the car pools!), and the glue that keeps the family together.

Though Tim and Jill clearly have a happy marriage, they do have a problem with communication.

She doesn't understand how a man like Tim thinks; he doesn't understand women at all. She wants to solve problems by talking them through, he wants to rewire them. Both are loving parents to their kids, youngsters Brad, Randy, and Mark. Of course, Tim spends his time trying to instill his "ultra manly" spirit into them, while Jill aims to give them broader, more sensitive values.

In spite of their differences and attitudes, however, Tim and Jill provide a loving, secure home for their children. They may have conflicts—after all, there wouldn't be a show if they didn't!—but no matter how haywire things get, the audience never doubts their unconditional love and support for each other and their family.

With all these dynamics—power tools, parenting, and the modern male mystique—as its comic building blocks, *Hammer Time* aimed to be a heartfelt and funny family comedy. There were several real powers behind the show. One, executive producer Matt Williams, was particularly famous. He'd helped a stand-up comedienne then known as Roseanne Barr to become the star of her own hit sitcom, ABC-TV's *Roseanne*. After public disagreements with his prima donna star, however, Mr. Williams departed that show. Still, he and his partners, Carmen Finestra and David McFadzean, maintained that the concept of transforming a successful stand-up comic into a sitcom star was a valid one. (they were right, and in doing so, started a trend, later to include Jerry Seinfeld, Ellen DeGeneres, and Brett Butler of *Grace*

Under Fire) Back in 1991 they found their new fun-
nyman in Tim Allen.

Tim, then, was always the main force behind *Hammer Time*. Just as *Roseanne* was created for her,
Hammer Time was created for him; it's his stand-up
shtick it's based on. In other words, Tim *was* the
show; all other casting was done around him.

In truth, the concept of modern man's primal urge
to hammer and saw wasn't just a funny stand-up
act—it wasn't so far from Tim's sit-down real life
either. Even when the cameras aren't rolling, Tim
Allen is very much a Mr. Fix-It, who actually is ob-
sessed with cars, power tools, and appliances. He is
also a "twelve-year overnight success story" who,
though hilariously funny, certainly never foresaw a
career in show business.

Tim comes by his love for fooling with tools honestly. Born and raised in Denver, Colorado, his fond-
est memories are of Saturdays spent with his father,
Gerald, and four brothers at a nearby department
store. They'd head straight for the—you guessed it—
hardware section and stay for hours. "Each of us
boys had a toolbox," Tim tells, "and every Christmas
my mom would get us each a new tool."

Tim's contented childhood came crashing to an
abrupt end when his father was killed by a drunk
driver. The family, though devastated, didn't cave in
the face of grief and hardship. They relied on their
strong love for each other to get them through. "We
were each other's support group before we even
knew what a support group was," Tim, who was
eleven at the time, explains.

Several years later, upon his mother's remarriage, the family moved to Birmingham, Michigan, where Tim attended high school. Never much of an academic type, Tim did ace at least one subject every year. You guessed it—shop class! He also developed a passion for cars that remains unflagging. He once traded an entire summer's pay for a custom-built dune buggy.

In high school Tim was famous for something else as well—being the class clown. "If I didn't have something to be a smart aleck about, I wasn't happy," he remembers. Years later the character of Randy Taylor would be based in part on the young Tim Allen. In spite of all that goofing off, Tim not only managed to graduate but go on to Western Michigan University. Looking toward a career behind the camera, he majored in television production.

Odd jobs followed, including stints at a sports store and an advertising company. At the latter he worked his way up to producing commercials, and every once in a while, he would cast himself as a background extra in one of them. That, however, is not what led to his emergence as a performer. Instead, it was a dare.

"One night some friends and I were at The Comedy Castle, a Detroit club specializing in stand-up. It was open mike night—where anyone could go on stage and try to be funny—and one guy dared me to go up and tell some jokes." And because Tim has never been one to turn down a dare, an entire career was born. "I found that I really could make other people laugh," Tim says incredulously. "And I thought, hey this is cool."

Over the years, he developed his patter, testing different routines until he struck upon a winner: the macho man character. With his trademark grunts of "Aaarrgh! Aarrgh! Aarrgh!" he had audiences howling. "My comedy celebrates what's cool about guys," Tim has described. "Guys love brand names, especially tool brand names and big block motors. That's how men communicate. They do not say, 'That's a nice outfit.' They say, 'Is that your hemi out there?' knowing the other guy will understand ... but few women would." Tim's aim wasn't to belittle women but to point out and parody the differences between the sexes. His real-life experience in the "battle of the sexes" came not only from jousting with his four sisters (he's from a big family) but by this time with his wife, Laura. Learning about the parenting part came courtesy of their daughter Kady.

While working the stand-up circuit, Tim was discovered by a Disney executive who knew Matt Williams and his partners were on the prowl for comics with the potential to become TV stars. Although Tim was interested in television, he held out for the right project before signing on the dotted line. In the end, *Hammer Time* (soon to be called *Home Improvement*) was that show.

The role of Tim's smart, spunky wife, Jill, required an actress of varied skills. She'd have to wield the real power around the house, but be sensitive enough not to come off bossy. Jill may rule the household, but always with a loving hand. She'd have to be a competent woman, but one audiences could relate to. In other words, not too perfect.

Patricia Richardson filled the bill. Herself a mother (of three, including infant twins) and wife (to actor Ray Baker), she was already an expert at juggling career with car pools, diapers with dialogue and a loving marriage. An accomplished actress, Texas-bred Pat cut her dramatic teeth on stage work and TV commercials before getting regular work on TV series. A veteran of three failed sitcoms—*Double Trouble, Eisenhower & Lutz,* and *FM*—she'd just about given up on TV altogether to concentrate on plays when *Home Improvement* came along.

It was completely by chance that she actually got the role—the original actress chosen for the part dropped out at the last minute—and by circumstance that she decided to take it. Also, as Pat cheerfully puts it, "At the time, I'd just given birth to twins and was too fat to play anything else!" Although she has slimmed down over the years, in the beginning, Pat was carrying an extra few pounds, which made her even more perfect for the purposely imperfect Jill. After all, what American working wife and mother can't relate to being a few pounds heavier than she'd like to be? In casting Patricia Richardson, there was an extra bonus: the warm familiarity and chemistry between herself and Tim was instantaneous and natural. The two were pals from the get-go and remain so today. That affection plays well on screen.

The roles of the Taylor sons were delineated somewhat less clearly than those of the parents. That

was partly because they were thought of as support-
ing roles, even less important than those of handy-
man Al (played brilliantly by Richard Karn), or the
wise but never fully seen neighbor, Wilson (the wry
Earl Hindman). At that stage in the show's development, no one even considered that any of the *boys*
would become a star.

As comic foils for Jill and especially Tim, there
were to be three of them and fairly close in age. As
the show began, they were about six, eight, and ten
years old. Mark, the youngest, was described as the
one who idolizes his know-it-all dad and wants to be
just like him. Brad, the oldest, was supposed to be
the sports-crazy kid on the brink of being girl-crazy.
Brad related to his dad with an interest in (if not an
identical passion for) cars and tinkering.

And then there was the middle son, Randy. When
Jonathan tried out for the role, the character was
described as "always in the middle of things, he's the
family troublemaker." Randy shared Tim's smart-
aleck sensibilities, but not his mechanical sense. An
artist, magician, and computer buff, he had not a
whit of interest in building or repairing anything, un-
less it was a scheme. Randy Taylor was a rascal, and
a smart one to boot. He earned A's on his report
card, while blustery brother Brad's cards said "needs
improvements." The two of them, however, put their
heads together when it came to teasing Mark—like
flushing his tadpole down the toilet or delivering the
news bulletin that, in fact, there was no Santa Claus.

Even though he was only ten, he understood the
character he'd be trying out for. "Randy is the mid-

dle son," he described. "He has two parents and a very loving home. He realizes he's secure, but he's still insecure in a way. He feels he *has* to joke around. That's how he relates to people. He's also a huge con artist. He's always getting into mischief, his wheels are always turning."

There's one obvious reason Jonathan could be so clear about the character. Bright, athletic, clever, and articulate, Randy really wasn't all that unlike Jonathan himself. Of course, there were differences. True, cutting up came naturally, but Jonathan also knew when to stop and get down to business: his teachers attest to that. And though no one can think up and deliver a one-liner faster and funnier, Jonathan also has a sensitive, caring side. His jokes never were at the expense of someone else.

As Jonathan analyzes it, "I think we're alike, because I also get into mischief, but I'm a good kid. I'm also a good student, but I do like to scheme. I'm always thinking about the next thing I can do—but I would never take things to the extent that Randy does." Though he doesn't have a younger brother, he's especially considerate of younger kids: he'd never act the way Randy does toward Mark.

Just because Jonathan knew he was perfect as the raspy, rascally Randy, however, didn't mean he was able to nail it right out of the gate. Hundreds of boys were tested, not only for his part but for the roles of Brad and Mark too. Groups of young hopefuls were asked to act out scenes alone, and then with two other boys. Producers were not only looking for a trio of talented tykes but three who looked and acted enough alike to be believable as brothers. It wasn't an easy task. As the months-long casting process wore on, the choices were whittled down as the finalists were called back to test again and again in different combinations. In all, JTT was called back four separate times. At the end of his fourth audition, he was given the news he'd been hoping to hear: he'd won the role of Randy Taylor.

He won it mainly because of his irresistible look, comic timing, and natural acting ability. But there was another reason Jonathan was chosen, and he freely admits it. "I do resemble Tim Allen," he said on a national talk show, "I saw the other kids who auditioned, and it was obvious—all of them looked kind of similar, as if they could be Tim's son, or least a part of the family." He added. "I think I have similar characteristics to Tim."

Speaking of the other boys who tried out, Jonathan first met Zachery Ty Bryan and Taran Noah Smith during the audition process. As he got to know them a little bit, he was surprised to find out that Zach, who'd won the role of Brad, was actually younger than he was by one month. Of course, Zach was quite a bit taller than Jonathan and, for sitcom purposes at least, did look older. Because they were so close in age and would soon be playing brothers, Jonathan and Zach bonded immediately.

Just as Jonathan was a perfect fit for Randy, so Zach was Brad to the bone. Cheerful, outgoing, and optimistic, Zach was an accomplished athlete, popular with guys and girls alike. An older brother in real life (to sister Ciri) he, too, comes from a loving, two-parent household not so very unlike the Taylors.

There were *some* differences between young actor and character, though. As Zach explained, "I am athletic, but I'm more sensitive and caring about other people's feelings than Brad sometimes is. Besides, at school I'm an A student and I'm not a brat." If Zach could improve his character in one way, he wouldn't tinker with his mischievous streak, but make him smarter, in school and at home. In the Taylor household it's Randy who's the leader and Brad the follower: Randy thinks up the schemes, and Brad goes along with them. That's not the case off-camera, where, as Zach points out, "I definitely consider myself a leader."

Zach took his first crack at showbiz before he was old enough to really know what it was all about. Born and mostly raised in Denver, Colorado, he was, like Jonathan, an adorable baby, wide-eyed and talkative, the type everyone said should be in front of the cameras. By the age of three he was. Picked to pose for a newspaper advertisement, Zach's too cute, happy face was the talk of the neighborhood. The little guy thrived on all the attention. A few years later, while watching children like himself in TV commercials, Zach was inspired to give that a try, too. "I said to my mom, 'I can do that—I *want* to do that.'" Lucky for him, mom Jenny, a former gymnast, was listening. She signed him up with a local talent agency, and the blond, blue-eyed seven-year-old got his start in local commercials.

A few summers after he'd begun, Zach attended

a camp for aspiring young performers. There he was discovered by a New York talent agent and soon signed up for more acting roles. His biggest, before *Home Improvement,* was a TV movie called *Crash: The Mystery of Flight 1501.* So much did Zach enjoy acting, that he decided—with his parents' consent and support, of course—to go to Los Angeles and try out for parts in TV series and movies.

Winning the role of Brad meant major changes in his life and that of his entire family because it meant pulling up stakes and moving from Denver to Los Angeles. It meant changing schools and soccer teams—for Zach has always been as devoted to that sport as he is to acting—leaving all his friends and cousins behind to form new relationships.

When he started on *Home Improvement,* Zach felt a little like a "stranger in a strange land." Although Jonathan had been in Los Angeles a bit longer, he had left family and friends behind in his hometown, too. That is one of the reasons the boys reached out to each other and became friends.

With Jonathan and Zach set as the older Taylor boys, that left the part of the baby of the brood, Mark, to complete the picture. After testing tons of youngsters, the one who came out ahead of the pack was Taran Smith, barely seven years old. He may have been the youngest, but Taran was actually the only one whose family had some showbiz savvy. His mom, Candy, worked as a script supervisor for movies. Not that Taran got the part because of it; his look and his natural abilities won him his role. But he did get started just by being around his mom's work. As a baby, Taran was a model for kids' magazines and clothing catalogs. He made the switch to commercials but had never been a regular on a TV show until *Home Improvement.*

Taran might have had a bit more showbiz savvy than either Jonathan or Zach, but he also had to move away from home (at least temporarily) to costar as Mark. Taran, who actually lived on a boat built by his father for the first four years of his life, is a native of San Francisco. Like the bigger boys, he had no friends in Los Angeles. But because of the three-year difference in their ages, Taran didn't immediately become as close to them. Eventually, though, he formed a tight bond with Zach.

Like the others, Jonathan and his family had a decision to make: whether to move permanently to Los Angeles or continue to try and maintain two households.

When Jonathan got his first series, *The Bradys,* he and his mom weren't so sure that a permanent move to Los Angeles was the right thing to do in such an uncertain business. And as it turned out, *The Bradys* wasn't to be a long-lasting gig.

But by the time *Home Improvement* came along, things had changed. It wasn't so much that JTT knew the show would be a hit—no one did. Jonathan recalls, "The script made me laugh, but no one knew if that meant the show would be successful." He figured that it probably *would* appeal to a wide audience, "People can relate to the struggles between siblings and the parent issues," as he put it. But that still wasn't a formula for great ratings.

Even ABC, the network that picked it up, couldn't predict its popularity. Although each actor was required to sign the standard seven-year contract, it's doubtful many thought it would last that long. In showbiz speak, Jonathan confides, "They only guaranteed us seven episodes." As he well knew, that wasn't much of a commitment, based on the twenty-six episodes that make a full season.

At the time, it was believed that *Home Improvement* would succeed or fail based on America's appetite for Tim Allen's comedy. But since humor is so subjective, no one could really predict if enough people would find it funny enough to keep on the air.

Knowing all that, Jonathan and his family decided to move. In the end, it had less to do with Jonathan's career than with the family's domestic situation, which had gone through some tough times. In 1990 Jonathan's parents had separated. By 1991 they were divorced. While his dad elected to stay up in the Sacramento area, there seemed to be no reason for the rest of the family to be there. After much discussion, Claudine, Joel, and Jonathan made the decision to move permanently. A change of scenery and lifestyle could be the best thing for all of them. Jonathan had already established himself in the industry and was happy. Even if *Home Improvement* didn't work out, by now it was clear that Jonathan had something very special to offer the entertainment industry; if he wanted to, he'd always be working. Claudine was thinking about putting her own career on hold to manage Jonathan's. If the show was a hit, she'd have to: who else was going to accompany him during his ten-hour day and look out for his welfare? And they had every expectation that Joel, while never interested in showbiz, would also settle into a new life in southern California.

They began by scouting out neighborhoods in which to settle. It didn't take long before they found exactly what they wanted: an area in the San Fernando Valley that boasted a top school district and competitive sports program, yet wasn't so far from Hollywood that Jonathan couldn't commute to work.

They were lucky enough to find a beautiful house that suited their needs perfectly. On a wide, tree-lined street, it was a split-level with a fireplace in the living room and swimming pool in the back. Each boy had his own bedroom, and Jonathan got to work immediately decorating his. He put up shelves and lined them with his growing baseball card and soccer trophy collections plus souvenirs from his fishing expeditions, including a stuffed yellowtail he'd caught on vacation in San Diego. He taped posters to the walls; some depicted calm, aquatic scenes; others were action shots of his favorite sports heroes.

The most important aspect of Jonathan's new life was that it never be too one-sided. "When I got into this business," Jonathan tells, "my mom was worried that I wouldn't have enough free time to be a kid, so there's always a balance between work and play."

Jonathan honestly feels that showbiz kids who don't have a balanced life are the ones who get into trouble down the road. As he told a newspaper journalist, "You have these kid actors who grew up and eventually go on *Geraldo,* crying that they never had any time, that they were totally corrupted by this business. Probably most of them didn't have much to fall back on. It's easy to get twisted in this business."

To make sure he had something to fall back on and didn't get "twisted," school naturally became a big part of the equation. When Jonathan got the role in *Home Improvement* and the family moved, he was in the middle of third grade. It's never easy changing schools in the middle of the term; no one, after all, likes to be "the new kid" when everyone else has already made friends. But if anyone could weather the discomfort of breaking into a new crowd, it was friendly, outgoing Jonathan. He entered third grade at a Los Angeles area public school in February, by March, he'd made friends who considered him "just one of the guys."

Academically, he had no problems either. Immediately put into the school's program for gifted children, Jonathan nevertheless worked hard at maintaining an A average. "I keep my grades up because you never know how your acting career is going to go," he told a reporter. To another he said, "Acting careers don't last a lifetime, so you ride it out and get the best education you can." Career or not, chances are Jonathan would have kept his grades up anyway: not only is he truly brilliant, he has a burning desire to learn about new things. And he cares. He likes to be a winner—academically and athletically.

Speaking of athletics, Jonathan signed up for his new town's soccer league, the Shockers, as well as their basketball team. He was welcomed to both; his ability and his spirit were appreciated. Never did Jonathan want to stand out as the TV-star player on any team. He tried hard, as he did in school, to be just one of the kids, accepted for his personality, friendship, and ability.

There was perhaps one thing Jonathan and his family were missing in their new digs—a couple of pets. McCormick, nicknamed Mac, a Lhasa apso puppy soon became a member of the family. He even had his own doghouse built in the backyard. While Joel bonded with Mac right away, Jonathan's heart was stolen by a Himalayan kitten named Samantha, who has always been called Sami.

Normal home life, as JTT would know it for the next couple of years, had begun.

Over at Disney, things were progressing behind the scenes as well, as the new comedy was getting ready to debut. First, there was some tinkering done with its name. The show that had started out on paper as *Hammer Time* went through two incarnations before becoming the one audiences are familiar with. *Hammer Time* went out the window before the pilot was filmed; afterward, it was known as *Tool Time*. After much discussion among the show's creators, Disney TV, Tim Allen, and The ABC network, it was decided that Tim's fictional cable show would retain the *Tool Time* title, while the show as a whole was rechristened *Home Improvement*.

There was a bit of fine-tuning done with the boys' names as well. Jonathan had been using "Taylor Thomas" as his professional name ever since he became an actor. Zach's real full name is Zachery Ty

Bryan, and that's how he'd always been billed. Whether it's because he felt left out, or was just trying to keep up, at the last minute, Taran added Noah—his real middle name—to his stage name.

This inevitably led to some carping by critics: "Three boys; nine names." There was more criticism to come, but in the end, none of it would amount to a hill of beans. *Home Improvement* would overcome that and a whole lot more.

HANGIN' WITH THE
HOME BOYS

In the early summer of 1991, Jonathan and the rest
of the cast began working on their new sitcom. The
series was slated for the 9:00 P.M. Tuesday night time
slot right between ABC's established comedies, *Full
House* and *Roseanne*. Why so late? Initially *Home
Improvement* was not thought of as a kids' show
since the comedy was built around Tim Allen's
"more power macho man" stand-up comedy routine.
The target audience was thought to be male adults
who would relate to Tim's "Mr. Fix-It" comedy
image. It was hoped that women would also tune in
just to see how Jill, played by Patricia Richardson,
really ruled the roost. Though Tim's character is
often puffed-up being a "manly-man," Patricia's role
shows her doing a balancing act looking for a job,
maintaining a home, and raising a family. There are

40

times when Jill and Tim argue and it seems that, they don't even speak the same language! But throughout, their love and affection for each other is always obvious.

As it happened, *Home Improvement* appealed to all audiences—old, young, male, and female. Patricia's take on *Home Improvement*'s universal appeal is that it reflects the reality of the typical American home and family, it isn't an idealized version. "If things between Tim and Jill get too soft," she explained, "then it's not as real as what happens in the audience's homes, and that's what they're responding to."

An added attraction for the male audience was Pamela Anderson, who was the first "Tool Time Girl" before she traded her hammer and nails for a bathing suit and full-time beach duties on *Baywatch*.

On September 17, 1991 *Home Improvement* joined the ABC fall lineup. It was an instant smash, landing at number nine on the Top Ten list of TV shows after its *first* broadcast. That proved to be no fluke. In a matter of weeks, it was obviously a solid hit with TV reviewers and critics scrambling to analyze its appeal. *Time* magazine explained *Home Improvement* "combines the ironic edge of Allen's stand-up comedy with traditional family-show sentimentality. ... [It] is a show about men, or more precisely about maleness. Tim is a swaggering takeoff on a macho guy who gets his kicks from rebuilding closets and working on his hot rod at 4 A.M."

At the end of its first season, *Home Improvement* was rated the number one new TV series, beating out all the others that had debuted that fall. Overall it was listed as number five on the official Nielsen Chart. Its popularity was further recognized when *Home Improvement* won the 1992 People's Choice Award for "Favorite New Comedy Series" and was nominated for an Emmy Award in the "Best Comedy" category.

Though it remained unacknowledged, the main reason for the unexpected popularity with a youthful audience was the three sons, Brad, Randy, and Mark. Kids immediately took to the cool, but not too bright, Brad, the mischief-making Randy, and the picked-on baby of the clan, Mark. Though the three child actors—Zachery, Jonathan, and Taran—were all adorable, it was JTT who seemed to ignite that special spark with the audience and fans.

Jonathan was finally doing what he had dreamed of for all these years—he was on a successful TV sitcom, entertaining millions of people every week. When *Home Improvement* made its first season debut, JTT had just celebrated his tenth birthday. Despite his youth and inexperience on a TV series, his adjustment to the daily routine was quite smooth. Most importantly, he understood his character even better now that he was actually playing him. "I'm like Randy because we're both always thinking and scheming," Jonathan revealed in one of his first interviews for *Kidsday,* a section of the New York newspaper, *Newsday.* "I have an older brother, so I am always trying to find ways to get back at him for things he did to me." Of course, there are some things Randy got away with on reel life that JTT

42

wouldn't try in real life. "I would never go as far as Randy does," he continued, referring to a silly sibling squabble on *Home Improvement*. "Like, I couldn't put my sixteen-year-old brother in a garbage can!"

Jonathan did admit that the grind of a weekly series was tough—but there was a major upside. In one of his first press conferences at the Disney studios, he told reporters: "It's fun, but it's work; everybody's always anxious to get things done on time. You have deadlines, you have cues, but you meet a lot of new people like Tim Allen, who's a great guy, and Patricia Richardson and the rest of the cast—don't let me forget anyone! It's just a real nice set to work on."

Jonathan's life began to take on a familiar pattern, divided between "work" days and "off" days. The *Home Improvement* schedule was an easy one to adapt to: three weeks on, one week off, starting at the end of July or early August and ending for hiatus in March or April. On the days Jonathan's required to be on the set, he wakes up at 7:00 A.M.—"without an alarm clock!"—and is ready by 8:00 A.M. for the hour-long ride to the Disney Studios in Burbank. While Claudine drives and country music plays on the radio, JTT busies himself reading the sports section of the newspaper or sometimes the classified ads. As he told *Disney Adventures* magazine: "I love old cars, so I like to see what's for sale. I like the '65 Mustang, the '54 Porsche Speedster, the '58 and '61 Chevy Impala—they're big boats, but they're cool." On other commutes, he goes over that week's script. Some people think it must be difficult memorizing all the lines for each show, but it comes naturally to Jonathan. "Once you get into the rhythm of reading the script, you can interpret it very easily," he explains. "The only problem is when the writers keep changing the lines, then I have to remember the new ones."

Depending on the traffic and how badly the L.A. freeways are backed up, Jonathan arrives at Stage 4 of the Disney Studios around 9:00 A.M. That's where he meets Zach and Taran in the on-set school trailer. By law, the kids are required to do three hours of school every day. They are taught all the appropriate subjects for their respective grades by a special on-set tutor who gets the class work from the boys' regular schools.

"In the morning we do an hour of school," Jonathan explains, "then rehearsals start. On Mondays we have what's called a table reading where producers and everyone in the cast sits around a table and reads over the script to see if it's funny, if the jokes are good, if the script comes together."

After the read-through, it's back to school for the boys while the rest of the cast continues rehearsal until lunch break. Everyone either drops by the Disney commissary for their midday meal or picks up something from the catering service table on the set. Since Jonathan is a vegetarian, he usually sticks to fruits, vegetables, soups, or pasta for lunch. However, the food selections in the cafeteria don't vary too much, and Jonathan admits he sometimes gets "sick of it, so I go to the health food store for variety." He also tries to squeeze in some extra study time during this break because he's determined his schoolwork is not going to suffer because of his career. The rest of the day is broken up between more school, more rehearsals, and staging the exact positions of the actors on the set.

As the week progresses, the show gets closer and closer to a finished product. Tuesday and Wednesday are devoted exclusively to rehearsals. By Thursday everything should be almost perfect—all script changes made, new scenes added, and those that aren't working cut. Then it's dress rehearsal. That's when JTT and the rest of the cast first put on the clothes selected by the wardrobe department for that particular episode. "They supply all the clothes," explains JTT, "but if there is something we don't like, we do have a say. . . . I'm allowed to tell them the clothes I like."

Monday through Thursday, Jonathan heads home around 6:00 P.M., and he usually does his homework during this end of the commute. But if he's caught up, he reads auto and fishing magazines and just chats away with his mom.

Friday is tape day, Jonathan's favorite day of the week. Actually, like most sitcoms, *Home Improvement* has two tapings on Friday, first in the afternoon and then later in the evening. The cast spends the morning and late afternoon having their makeup and hair done, going over last-minute changes, and wishing each other luck. Although JTT is always prepared, he admits he has occasional butterflies on tape day. "You can do this a million times, and you are still going to be nervous because you can't beat stage fright," he says. "Sometimes I [go to my dressing room] and watch TV to mentally take that pressure away."

Part of the pressure, of course, is taping in front of a live audience, but once Jonathan gets on the set, all those butterflies fly away. He thrives on the give-and-take of actor and audience and says: "I love performing in front of an audience. . . . I like to hear the reaction of real live people. [Since] the show is taped before a live audience, all the laughs are real. We have microphones that hang out over the audience and pick up the laughs. . . . It's much better than a laugh track."

Actually, in those early days there were a lot of laughs on the set of *Home Improvement*—both in front of the audience and behind the scenes. The cast was close and the gregarious Jonathan made friends with everyone almost instantly. Jonathan even found common ground (or seas) with some of the crew members, especially those who share his love of fishing. "There are a couple of fishermen among the crew members on the set," Jonathan explains. "I like to sit back with them and swap exaggerated fish stories—I caught a . . . nine-footer! Oh yeah!"

In those early days, of course, his costars Zach and Taran had the most in common with JTT since the three were the only kids on the set. Though they'd originally bonded because none had real friends his own age in L.A., it didn't take long for JTT and Zach to find other common ground. Sports was a big link. Both Jonathan and Zach were serious sports fanatics and loved to play basketball, football, and especially soccer. In their respective Los Angeles areas, the first thing each had done after registering at school was join a soccer league. Between scenes they'd often kick a soccer ball around the Disney lot.

Besides sports, the two shared an impish sense of humor. Both were high-energy kids who loved to play pranks and dash around the set between takes—yet both could stop on a dime and be ready to deliver his lines on cue. And neither, of course, was very different from the character he was assigned to play—their roles seemed "Taylor"-made for them.

"Zach and I gravitate toward each other naturally," Jonathan once explained of his early relationship with his costar, adding in typical preadolescent fashion, "but I'm the oldest and the leader. I like that. I like being the leader. I may not be the biggest, but I can always say, 'I'm the oldest—we do this!' " Of course, Zach didn't always agree with that assessment.

And then there was Taran. On the show, as Mark, he's always being picked on and teased by his big brothers, but when the cameras turn off, things were a little bit different. JTT and Zach never ganged up on Taran. Like typical older brothers, there were times when they looked out for Taran and times they did their own thing. "We don't leave him out," supersensitive Jonathan said, "even though he's three years younger—that's a big difference in mentality and athletic ability. We're more coordinated, so when we play sports, we just pair him up with a bigger person."

Like all the actors on *Home Improvement,* each

of the boys had his own dressing room. A sign on Jonathan's door read "The Great Randini," and inside he plastered his walls with posters of his favorite baseball, basketball, and hockey players, as well as posters from cool movies like *Boyz 'n the Hood*. When you walked by JTT's home away from home in those days, you heard music constantly. At the time, he was into rap and the sweet harmonies of Boyz II Men.

During the show's first few years Zach's and Taran's rooms were situated right next door to Jonathan's, making it that much easier for the boys to hang out together. Truth is, the guys had gotten so tight, they used to cut up behind the scenes constantly, running around the set, whooping and hollering. It got to the point where they'd earned themselves the reputation as the "Home Imps!" That not entirely positive image became a little more public when *Entertainment Tonight* did one of its first behind-the-scenes pieces on the show. "*ET* came in and made it look like we were little monsters," Jonathan said later, "when we're really just *active*, energetic normal kids." It wasn't a big deal, but it was the first time Jonathan was surprised at the power of the press to misrepresent him. It wouldn't be the last time.

All three boys had something else in common. Since all were minors, they were required by law to have a guardian on the set at all times. Most of the time it was their moms—Claudine for JTT, Jenny for Zach, and Candy for Taran. The young mothers gravitated toward each other in much the same way their sons had. Since each woman had another non-professional child at home to take care of also (Jonathan's brother Joel, Zach's sister Ciri, and Taran's sister Aria), they often would take turns watching each other's boys on the set.

By the end of the first season of *Home Improvement*, it was obvious that Tim Allen, who has a real-life five-year-old daughter, had developed a close relationship with his TV sons. But insiders insist that there was something very special between Tim and Jonathan from the beginning. Perhaps because Zach and Taran live with both parents, unlike Jonathan, who by that time wasn't seeing much of his dad, Tim took more of an interest in JTT. For though it was under different circumstances, Tim also lost his dad when he was young, so he understood how hard it can be on a boy not to have a father figure. Of course, it could also be that Tim and JTT naturally share the same wise-cracking sense of humor! Whatever the reason, it was clear from day one that Jonathan adored and admired Tim—and was his best audience—and Tim took Jonathan under his wing.

Once you get Jonathan started talking about Tim Allen, it's almost as if he can't stop. "He's been doing stand-up for years," JTT told a magazine reporter, "and sometimes acts as if our cast and crew is his own little private theater. He never stops with the one-liners—it's like he's doing an act twenty-four hours a day!"

Though to some, it seemed like a laughathon between Tim and Jonathan, others noticed that the young actor was absorbing a great deal about being a professional from his mentor. Jonathan soon learned there were times to kid around and other times to get busy. "Tim blows his lines the most, but it may be deliberate—he's a very funny guy," Jonathan continued with his Allen analysis. "Tim keeps everybody loose on the set. You can threaten Tim with the worst of things, and he'll still turn it into a joke. He's amazing, but at the same time very professional, gets his work down. He's the loosest, mellowest guy you'll ever know—a blast to work with."

Tim and Jonathan's offscreen relationship mirrors their father-son image on screen. And if Brad is the son Tim's TV character is close to because of a shared interest in cars and all things mechanical, it is JTT who really shares his *offscreen* sense and sensibilities: of humor and intellect. Tim has really taken Jonathan under his wing, and there is definitely one person who is very grateful—JTT's mom, Claudine.

"Tim Allen is a big help," she explained to a national magazine. "He keeps an eye on Jonathan and takes a special interest. Tim knows that Jonathan's dad and I are divorced, and his dad, who lives in Sacramento, doesn't see him a lot. Tim helps keep Jonathan's head from swelling. If he sees any ego flaring, he playfully teases Jonathan."

If on the set of *Home Improvement* it was Tim Allen who helped keep life normal for Jonathan that first season, at home it was all up to Claudine. She was determined not to let Hollywood change her young son, so he definitely didn't get the star treatment there. As in any household, Claudine assigned both her kids duties. "I have my chores to do," Jonathan described to a reporter. "I have to make my bed and vacuum the pool. I've gotta make sure the litter boxes are clean and that my cats and dog have fresh food and water. And I take the trash out."

But once that was out of way, and all his homework done, Jonathan enjoyed himself like any other kid. During weekends, hiatus time, and vacations he went to L.A. Dodger baseball games (he even caught a ball at one!), went fishing, watched his favorite TV shows like *Full House, Roseanne, Who's the Boss?* and *Growing Pains,* and played sports whenever he could. Even for Jonathan, though, there was some quiet time, and that was when he loved to lose himself in books like *Hatchet, James and the Giant Peach,* and *Island of the Blue Dolphin.*

Another one of Jonathan's favorite pastimes was adding to his collection of sports cards and soccer pins, some of which were from teams as far away as Russia, Australia, and Germany. Actually Jonathan's bedroom was looking more and more like a huge sports memorabilia showcase. Naturally that Dodger baseball went right into his collection, as did the various autographed cards and balls he amassed. Tim Allen even made a contribution when he got running back Barry Sanders of the Detroit Lions to sign a football for Jonathan. Of course, Jonathan's celebrity did help a bit. "I did a photo shoot with Dennis Eckersley of the Oaklands A's, and he signed a ball for me," Jonathan recalled. "I also met Reggie Jackson and Kareem Abdul-Jabbar, and they signed balls for me."

Adjusting to an entire new lifestyle in Los Angeles

wasn't always easy, however, and there were times when work spilled over into Jonathan's playtime. But on such occasions, as when he had to make personal appearances on weekends, he and his mom found a way to compensate for his loss of free time. They'd make what was essentially a "business thing" into something fun. Whenever they traveled they'd check out all the historical and geographical points of interest and history buff Jonathan began to look forward to those excursions.

Jonathan's favorite time off the set of *Home Improvement*, though, was when he hung out with his friends—his non-showbiz pals from school and his soccer teammates. "I really prefer just being a regular guy," Jonathan has said. "When I first got to the school, not many kids knew me, so they asked a lot of questions. It was a little difficult in the beginning. Most of the kids are very nice, and I haven't had any problems. Sometimes they'll talk about last night's episode of the show or something—they might say, 'I didn't like those overalls you wore, they were dorky.' Or 'Hey, cool hat,' you know, stuff like that. I never mind, as long as it's not the whole conversation."

Still, Jonathan's closest friend at the time remained his on-screen brother, Zach. Even on weekends, Jonathan and Zach chose to get together. "We'd pop over to each other's houses and listen to music," JTT recalled.

More often than not, the two would be comparing soccer notes. Unfortunately, because of their schedules, neither could make all of the practices or games, but it was still very important to them. To Jonathan, belonging to a soccer team meant he could be "just one of the guys," that he wasn't singled out because he was on TV.

Similarly Jonathan preferred regular school to the tutoring he got on *Home Improvement*. By the time Jonathan was in the fourth grade, he was an old pro at splitting up his time and studies. "I love being on the set and doing work there, but I also love going back to the classroom and seeing my friends," he admitted to friends. "Also I like seeing the grass around the school. At work it's just asphalt—no fields to run in."

When the first season of *Home Improvement* ended, Jonathan was ready for a summer vacation, but when it came time to report back for the 1992–93 season, he was raring to go! *Home Improvement* started its second season on Wednesday, September 16th—same time, 9:00 P.M., but a new night, which turned out to be just the first of *many* changes for the cast on-screen and off. Jill Taylor got a job that season, requiring Tim to pitch in more with the household chores, which almost always led to a disaster since he wanted to apply "more power" to the simplest of tasks. Jill's mom was introduced on the show, giving Tim an on-screen mother-in-law. More laughs. Meanwhile, down on the set of *Tool Time,* Tim got a new boss—and it was a woman. His reaction? The typical "Arrggh! Arrggh! Arrggh"! Changes were in store for the boys as well. Randy got to fly as Peter Pan in a school play, which Tim nearly destroyed. Brad got interested in girls, and

Mark, well, he was still picked on by his older brothers.

Once again the series was pulling in huge ratings and Jonathan was getting more and more into his character. He had only one unfulfilled desire. "The only thing I wish is that they'd start getting him interested in girls. But I like Randy. I'm happy playing him."

Clearly the second season was a lot of fun for JTT. He laughed constantly at Tim's antics, never more so than when they taped an episode dealing with Tim's fears of snakes. Jonathan still refers to that episode as his all-time favorite. "That was very funny, especially when the snake, which was hiding in the wall behind the phone, slithered down Tim's shirt." Jonathan still feels the expression on Tim's face in that scene was one of *Home Improvement*'s classic moments.

It seemed that a lot of people tuned in for that episode—and all the others—because by the end of the second season, *Home Improvement* was a true TV phenomenon. Reportedly, it attracted thirty million viewers each week. Once again it was a winner at the People's Choice Awards, this time for Favorite Comedy Series and Tim received a nod as Favorite Male TV Performer. The show also garnered five Emmy nominations and ended the season in the number three place on the Nielsen charts. It also made TV history when it was given a three-year renewal by ABC in an unprecedented vote of confidence. It was a good move by the network—*Home*

Improvement attracted *twice* as many men, women, *and* children as any other sitcom at the time.

When asked why he thought *Home Improvement* had taken the nation by storm, Tim Allen modestly responded: "The show's special because of the chemistry between cast members. It really becomes apparent when you watch it."

When the exhilarated cast celebrated their season "wrap party" on the *Home Improvement* set, everyone was talking about the vacations they were planning for that summer's hiatus. Everyone, that is, except Jonathan. He had *other* plans!

THE VOICE OF CHOICE!

For putting in two hectic seasons on *Home Improvement,* JTT was a showbiz pro—and really into the "work mode." He just didn't want to stop, and for the next couple of months, he didn't.

He appeared in the TV show "A Bush Gardens Sea World Special," which was filmed at the Florida theme park. It was a one-hour special about animals and taking care of endangered species. He hosted a cable special, *Wild and Crazy Kids,* and did a guest spot on Nickelodeon's *Double Dare* in Orlando, Florida. There, he and Zach got to meet and mingle with the cast of *The Mickey Mouse Club,* which was really cool. "We wanted to meet them, but they wanted to meet us, too," he gushed.

It was also during this hiatus that Jonathan got his first taste of lending his celebrity to charitable events and organizations. It was the first time that *his* participation might inspire people to donate money or work on behalf of a favorite charity. To young JTT, this was *by far* the coolest part of being a star. Two of his favorite events were the *Earthday Everyday* music video for the environmental organization EarthTrust, in which he appeared with thirty-six other young stars, and the SEGA Star Kids Challenge, which benefits a group of charities every year.

Something else happened during this hiatus. Jonathan got more involved in his "second career"—voice-overs. Many of Jonathan's fans don't realize he can be *heard* even more often than he can be seen. Jonathan, who'd started doing voice-overs for commercials and cartoons *before* he got on TV, was in constant demand.

It may sound simple, but doing voice-overs isn't always easy. When actors are working on TV or movies, they react to another person in the scene. When they do voice-overs, however, they are often in a room all alone with just a microphone, reading along with what's happening on the screen. It's a special skill that takes timing and a lot of practice to do it convincingly. The challenge has always appealed to Jonathan. "It is fun," JTT explained of the experience. "It's just you. The director and producers are on the other side of a glass wall, and you don't know what they're saying. So you don't know if you were good or horrible. But it's kind of cool because you don't have to depend on other people to get their lines right—it's all you." Starting with commercials, Jonathan has compiled an impressive body of work in that field.

The voice-over kid has many other animated

series/cartoons to his credit: *The Ivy Cottage, Chuck the Beaver,* and *Little Wizard Stories,* which is based on the *Wizard of Oz* books. The premise of these tales is that Dorothy, Scarecrow, Tin Man, and the Lion had children—the Oz Kids. There's Dot and her brother Neddy, the Tin Boy, two Lion Cubs, and a Scarecrow Junior—that's Jonathan. Right now *Little Wizard Stories* is being seen oversees but may appear on TV in the U.S. or be released on video.

He has starred in a four-volume video series based on the children's book character Spot, the dog. Originally published and translated to video in England, the stories are based on author Eric Hill's classic chronicles of Spot's adventures. Disney bought the United States' rights to the *Spot* videos and hired Jonathan to do the Americanized voice of the famous puppy. Aimed at preschoolers, the *Spot* videos are extremely popular.

Jonathan has also completed a CD-ROM game from Electronic Arts called *Scooter's Magic Castle.* Jonathan is the voice of Scooter. In this game, which is targeted at four- to seven-year-olds, Scooter has to explore a ghost-filled castle. Jonathan explained it to an interviewer, "It's a computer game—Scooter has a magic castle, and he takes you around it. It's real interesting. There is a typing program and a memorization program to help you [learn] easily. Also, it has songs you can write if you want to be a musician. It's nice because it has different levels of difficulty, so if you're not real experienced at this game, you can put it on the easy level and as you get better, increase it. Working on *Scooter* was great and a lot of fun. It's 'edutainment'—it provides education and entertainment at the same time."

Another one of Jonathan's most popular cartoon voices is the character George on the USA network's series, *The Itsy Bitsy Spider,* the tale of a little girl named Leslie who is befriended by a spider named Itsy. Russell Marleau, the producer of *The Itsy Bitsy Spider* recalled how Jonathan got involved with the series and even got his character, George, more work. "When the show began, we wanted our main characters, Itsy and Leslie, to meet a boy there that they could relate to. So we brought in a bunch of boy actors for auditions. We listened to them all, and I immediately recognized Jonathan's voice because I watch *Home Improvement.* I thought he'd be great. Everyone liked him, and anyone who'd seen *Home Improvement* also knew he could actually act. So we went ahead and cast him, and he was so good, we decided to use him as a recurring character. George sort of evolved. In the episodes he would be in, he and the little girl, Leslie, would go on adventures. George [is] a bit of a wimpy character. He's always holding back because he thinks things are getting too dangerous. So Leslie and Itsy are always encouraging him. We used George more because Jonathan was that good, and he was fun to work with. He's such a little professional."

Back *Home* Again

With all that voice-over work, before Jonathan turned around, it was time to go back to *Home Im-*

provement for season three, 1993–94. Well, not quite. There were a few things to iron out first. Unfortunately, they weren't pleasant.

The show itself was doing phenomenally well—better that ever, in fact. It had ended on a high note: the number three of all prime-time series. The writers, cast, and crew were "powered up" and ready to roll over the competition and make the new season the best ever.

As the third season began, the time slot for *Home Improvement*—Wednesday 9:00 P.M.—remained the same, but there *were* changes for the characters. In addition to her work as a researcher on *Detroit Magazine,* Jill Taylor got even busier with a library fundraiser project. And when her sister discovered she was pregnant with a girl, Jill contemplated adding a new member to the Taylor clan—maybe a girl, also. There were changes on the set of Tim's *Tool Time* show, too. Pamela Anderson left and was replaced by Debbie Dunning as the "Tool Time Girl." Tim's costar on the show, Al (Richard Karn), decided he wanted to settle down and get married, so the wife watch was on. Back at home, the boys started expressing their personalities more. Brad, who had begun junior high, signed up for home economics instead of shop and shocked everyone until Tim realized the method to his eldest son's "madness": there are more girls to meet in home economics than shop—*Arghhh!* Mark discovered that when Jill was pregnant with him, she wanted a little girl, and he questioned if he was a "disappointment." Randy turned into more of a rebel and, in an effort to appear "cool," started making his dad the butt of his jokes. The mood on the set was full of excited anticipation, and Executive Producer Carmen Finestra commented, "I'm hopeful our audience will continue to grow. The scripts are better than ever, and we think our third season is going to be our strongest yet."

It all sounded like a bang-up new season, but everything was almost put on hold. The reason centered around the boys. In a surprise move, all three—Zach, Taran, and JTT—did not show up for work on what should have been the first day on the set. Their absence led to much controversy, all of which was described in laborious detail in major newspapers and magazines around the country. Most of what made the papers, however, was pretty one-sided. All three boys were totally slammed for what was perceived as a "walkout." The reports made them look bad, while the more balanced real story was never really explained to the public.

The newspapers said the boys were "on strike" for "big raises" and, further, that one kid's dad demanded a part on the show. It was also stated that the boys wanted major "perks," that they didn't want to *walk* to the commissary for lunch while the adults had their food delivered. Zach, Taran, and JTT were portrayed as little ingrates, and one executive was quoted as saying: "Instead of being grateful for a successful show, they were asking 'How much more can we get?'." The boys were even dubbed "the brat pack" by some observers, and one of the showbiz Bibles, the *Hollywood Reporter,* claimed that the powers that be on *Home Improvement* were actually ready to replace the boys on the series and had gone so far as to put out casting calls.

The real story was very different. The boys and their families were concerned with issues of safety and health. Each day during lunch, the boys were allowed recreation time, but their designated area of play was actually the truck and fire lane outside the *Home Improvement* set! A basketball net was set up there and when the boys were shooting hoops, they had to watch out for delivery cars and trucks coming through. The boys and their parents had been lobbying for a safe area to play for two years—they still hadn't gotten it.

There was also a health concern for the past two seasons. The boys' three director's chairs were in a row next to their teacher, but the chairs themselves were chained together—with a lock. The result was that no matter what the circumstances, Zach, Taran, and JTT were practically on top of each other. If one had a cold or was somehow under the weather, the other two were exposed to his germs. If two of the boys had a spat and needed a little space from each other, it was impossible to get away. They wanted to be treated as individuals.

And they wanted to be treated with respect as professionals, too. All the adult actors had specific director's chairs assigned to them, with their names on the back. Between takes the boys sat in chairs with the logo "Home Improvement" on the back. It seemed as if they were considered interchangeable and not treated with respect.

For two years the boys' parents asked for remedies to these problems but received no response. At the beginning of the third season, the requests were renewed. As it turned out, Jonathan really was sick at the time. When the controversy broke out, Jonathan's manager explained, "My client has been ill, and we're hoping he recovers soon and reports back to work."

Though things finally worked out—the boys returned to the set, a new, safe play area was built, the chairs were unlocked, and each young actor's name was put on the back—Zach, Taran, and Jonathan still had some hurt feelings. The press reports made them look greedy and egomaniacal. No one had bothered to ask them for their side of the story, and only the teen magazines bothered to follow up. Later on, when Tim was queried about the problem, he shrugged it off because it was all after the fact. "It won't affect the show because by the time anybody knew about it, it was over," he said.

Ever the professional, Jonathan took the whole uncomfortable episode in stride. Once the adults had settled matters, there was no noticeable tension on the set because of the flap, and everyone picked up as before. *Home Improvement* went on to overpower the competition. Its third season, in fact, became its most successful ever. Some of the cast members turned this success into further stepping stones to individual fame and fortune. Tim Allen landed the lead in his first movie, *The Santa Clause,* which was a major box-office success. Patricia Richardson got nominated for an Emmy. Jonathan, though he hardly knew it would lead to his emergence as a superstar, landed a part in a movie that would end up being his *big* breakthrough.

Funny enough, it was voice-over, *not* a live action film. It was, however, a feature film, something Jonathan hadn't done before. It was, of course, *The Lion King*.

THE MANE EVENT

Jonathan has always been happiest when he's busiest and after several seasons of *Home Improvement,* he was pretty content. He thrived on his nonstop schedule that combined the show, voice-over work, charity functions, school, sports, and social life. To an outside observer, it seemed JTT didn't have time to even *think* about adding anything else to his routine. But when *The Lion King* roared, Jonathan listened. "I didn't expect ever in a million years to be doing TV *and* movies," Jonathan said with delight when he won the role of Simba, the son of the lion king, Mufasa.

If Jonathan was surprised about landing his role in *The Lion King,* it's pretty fair to say no one expected his first venture into feature films to become one of the all-time box-office mega-winners. Of course, from the very beginning *The Lion King* had the earmarks of being a major sensation. It was being released by Disney Pictures and from the same producers who had put together the smash hits *Beauty and the Beast* and *Roger Rabbit*. By the time Jonathan auditioned for the voice of Simba, some of Hollywood's biggest names had already signed on the dotted line: James Earl Jones, Matthew Broderick, Whoopi Goldberg, Cheech Marin, and Jeremy Irons. Music greats Elton John and Tim Rice had been commissioned to write the songs for the film. When Jonathan was asked why he wanted to add yet another project to his already heaping plate, he merely answered, "A lot of great actors [are involved]. It's a real, real nice film."

Actually Jonathan related to the character of Simba. "He is a lot like me," JTT explained. "[He's] real curious, fun-loving, always getting into mischief."

Not surprisingly, Jonathan felt that Simba was also similar to his *Home Improvement* character. "Simba and Randy are both curious kids, they're both intuitive and confident, always ready to throw that fast one in, that little comment," remarked JTT astutely.

Not only was *The Lion King* a "nice film" but it was new creative ground for Disney, the grandfather of all animation companies. *The Lion King* was the first Disney cartoon feature *not* based on an existing fable or a literary work, and it was the first time there were no human character or human influence in the story. However, there was one "first" on which Jonathan didn't want to take a chance—singing the songs! When he got the role of the speaking voice of Simba, he was also asked to audition for the songs young Simba performed. Jonathan's always up for a challenge, but he knows his limits. "I didn't do the singing," Jonathan explained quite candidly. "I can carry a tune, but not for anything that I would want millions of people to go see. [I told the producers] it won't be pretty."

Disney then turned to the young actor/singer Jason Weaver, who had appeared in the short-lived TV sit-com, *Thea,* and played the young Michael Jackson in a TV movie, to do the singing for the film. It was a perfect chance, since Jason has an incredible sing-ing voice, as well as talent to "match" it to Jona-than's speaking voice. Still Jonathan admitted that whenever he heard "Hakuna Matata," his favorite song from the movie, he sang along ... quietly!

There was no one, however, who was a better choice as Simba than Jonathan. "We had this role for a scrappy young kid to play Simba, and we looked at dozens and dozens of actors," recalled producer Don Hahn. But the funny thing was, in the end, they didn't have to look any further than across the way on the Disney lot! "We saw him on *Home Improve-ment* and just thought his voice was right," Hahn continued. "It gives him a very distinctive character."

What was Jonathan's response when he heard that his voice was one of the deciding factors to cast him as Simba? "My voice is just a regular kid's voice," he said with typical modesty, then added, "maybe kind of raspy. [The role] called for an energetic cock-iness. But I didn't have to invent a voice or anything. I just had to talk with a real kid spirit."

As an actor, Jonathan already was used to doing

certain voice exercises to strengthen its tone and timber. But when he took on the voice-over role of Simba, he had to protect his vocal cords even more than usual. A few things had to change. "When I'm playing soccer, I tend to yell and scream on the field," he admitted. "I wasn't able to do that anymore." And when he did strain his voice by overusing it, Jonathan soothed his throat with hot tea with lemon and honey.

Of course, it wasn't only Jonathan's voice that made him the perfect choice for Simba—it was his talent and his own spunky attitude. That attitude came in handy during the long recording and editing sessions over the next two years. It wasn't all fun and games, recalled producer Hahn only half jokingly in a *People* magazine profile on Jonathan. "We darn near beat [Jonathan] up when we were recording. We had to make it sound like he was being flung down chutes in the elephant graveyard and being chased by wildebeests. So we would rough him up at the microphone and try to make him out of breath."

There were times over the next two years when Jonathan claimed he didn't know if he was coming or going. Dividing his time for his personal life, *Home Improvement,* and Simba, he said, "I had to kind of go, 'Oops! Time to be Randy' ... 'Oops! Time to be Simba.' You have to prepare yourself to become this totally different person. I mean, we're not lions, right?"

The whole project was definitely a challenge, and though Jonathan was not unfamiliar with doing voice-overs, a Disney feature film like *The Lion King* was *major!* "I'm used to having all these other actors and actresses around on the set of *Home Improvement,*" Jonathan recalled of the time spent in and out of the soundproof booth from the fall of 1992 to the spring of 1994. "In this case, I didn't. I was in there in a room alone, and I not only had to play my character but [also] the people I was talking to. I had to get inside their heads so I could know what Simba would be reacting to. . . . I learned a lot about comic timing. And the nice thing about doing an animated film is that they're for all ages and all time."

Needless to say Jonathan and the other actors weren't the only ones putting in long hours and hard work. Over six hundred Disney illustrators created more than one million drawings for *The Lion King* over a period of three years. But whenever anyone who was connected with the film was asked what made it worth spending so much time and energy on *The Lion King,* almost everyone would say . . . "The story!"

Jonathan was no exception. He fell in love with the coming-of-age tale the minute he read the script. "It's about a place in Africa called the Prideland, and it takes place in this huge rock formation in the valley," Jonathan explained shortly after he began work on the project. "Simba is this lion cub and his dad, Mufasa [James Earl Jones], is the Lion King. Simba will become the king when he gets older, but his evil uncle Scar, [Jeremy Irons], wants to claim the throne for his own, and the only way to do that is to kill Mufasa and make Simba think it's his fault.

It's all about responsibility and life, kinda, what you have to go through, the challenges that you face. It's a very nice film. It's gonna be great."

Jonathan was right on the mark with that prediction!

With *The Lion King,* Jonathan entered a whole new world. The first step was doing the voice of Simba. He would go over to the Todd-AO Studios for his recording sessions. He would work an hour at a time in a soundproof cubicle, wearing giant headphones and speaking directly into the microphone. Everything had to be fit in around Jonathan's other commitments. "We were able to schedule an hour here, an hour there for me to record," he recalled. "It's amazing how much you can get done in an hour."

The recording in Los Angeles was only part of the job—there was more to do in Orlando, Florida. When Jonathan flew to the Disney/MGM Studios, he was treated like a prince. He got to meet the main *Lion King* animators. Chief animator Mark Henn videotaped Jonathan during several recording sessions so the artists could use his facial expressions and body language as a guide when they drew Simba. "The animators are incredible," Jonathan said when he returned from Florida. "They videotape your face as you're reading, and then they take your expressions and put them into the drawing. It's so cool. You can see some of my expressions in Simba, like when he gets scared and stuff."

Besides the videotaping, Jonathan had to sit for a photo session for headshots so each of the animators could work from it when they were drawing Simba. They must have captured that special JTT quality because many of the reviews of the movie mentioned that Simba's expressive face seemed almost human.

The Lion King premiered in Hollywood on June 17, 1994. Jonathan was front and center, participating in all the special events surrounding the film. The funny thing is, it was at the premiere that Jonathan met his costars for the first time. "I never had the pleasure of working with them," he recalled, since all of the actors had done their voice-overs just as Jonathan had—alone in sound booths. But after the movie opened across the country and started getting rave reviews, Jonathan saw his fellow actors a number of times—mostly at awards shows.

The night of the premiere itself was everything Hollywood is famous for—glitz, glamour, global attention. Celebrities arrived and were interviewed and photographed by journalists and paparazzi from all over the world. Everyone knew from the minute the opening credits rolled that *The Lion King* was going to break all records. But on a more personal level, Jonathan and his mom watched the culmination of two years work, the results of cross-country efforts on the part of the young actor. And they were pleased.

"When I saw the movie with my mother, she said, 'That's what you do when you get sad. That's what you do when you're happy.' It's pretty cool to be immortalized in a Disney classic!" Jonathan said after *The Lion King*'s premiere.

The Lion King grossed $42 million on its opening

weekend. Throughout the summer and fall of 1994, *Lion King* mania swept the country, even the world. The film broke all box-office records, but that was just the tip of the iceberg. Kids everywhere were acquiring *Lion King* merchandise—from lunch boxes to Halloween costumes—like nothing before. Then, just in time for the Christmas holidays' spending spree, *The Lion King* was re-released in November of 1994. At latest count *The Lion King* soundtrack album sold more than seven million copies, and over one billion dollars in officially licensed products were sold.

As 1995 arrived, *The Lion King* proved it was not just a flash in the pan, not just last year's headlines. It created all-time records. It grossed $751 million at the box office worldwide. Of course, it was the biggest animated film that ever hit the theaters, but it also made more money in 1994 than *any* other film (not just animated); it joined *E.T.* and *Star Wars* as the top moneymaking films ever; it earned twice as much as Hollywood's "experts" had predicted. And that was just the beginning. The award shows began.

In January 1995 *The Lion King* walked away with Golden Globes for Best Musical Comedy Film and Best Original Song—"Can You Feel the Love Tonight." In February "Circle of Life" and "Can You Feel the Love Tonight" were nominated for Best Song of the Year at the Grammys. In March *The Lion King* won Oscars for Best Original Score for songwriter Hans Zimmer and Best Original Song for "Can You Feel the Love Tonight" by Elton John and Tim Rice.

Also in March of 1995 *The Lion King* video was released and quickly became the fastest selling home-viewing movie ever. It shattered all records, selling over twenty million copies in less than a week. It far surpassed even Disney's other major video releases: *Snow White, Aladdin, Beauty and the Beast.* And it's still not over—there are plans to release a sequel to *The Lion King* direct to video in 1996.

All the success of *The Lion King* would make anyone's head spin, but Jonathan, who received rave reviews for his work on the film, took it all in stride. "When I did it, I had some idea it would be a success because of Disney's long-term success with animated pictures," he said. But Jonathan had no idea just what an effect *The Lion King* would have on him both professionally and personally. He was soon to find out.

MAN OF THE HOUSE

One thing that had not changed was the success of *Home Improvement* and its star. Even with its rocky start, the show finished the third season as the number one prime-time series, Tim Allen was the most popular male star on TV, and Jonathan had become the top teen star.

As the summer hiatus was nearing, everyone wanted to know what the most popular teenager on the number one show was going to do with his time off. When Jonathan was queried about his future plans, he told a reporter, "I'd love to do a movie. That would be great. It depends upon the timing, because we have a very short amount of time when the show is on hiatus, but if the dates work out, then great, but if they don't, then no. But I'd love to do a movie."

Of course, if a movie didn't come along, JTT was prepared. "I'll probably just hang out with my

Photo by Anthony Cutajar

The "Home Imps" circa 1992:
JTT, Taran Noah Smith, and
Zachary Ty Bryan.

JTT!

Photo by Ann Bogart

"I wish I could write everyone back," says Jonathan as he pores over his fan mail.

JTT's got more logo hats than any other kid around!

Photo by Anthony Cutajar

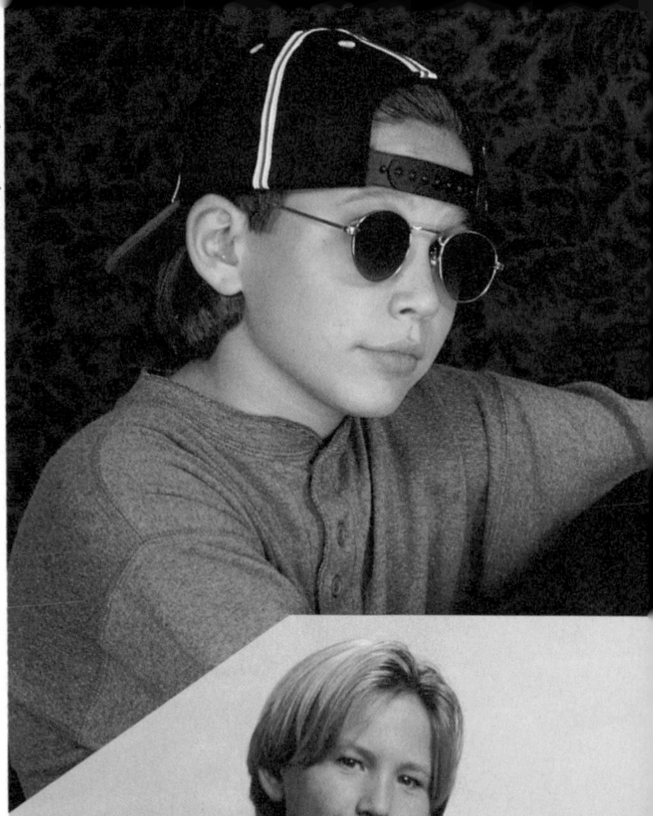

Photo by Ann Bogart

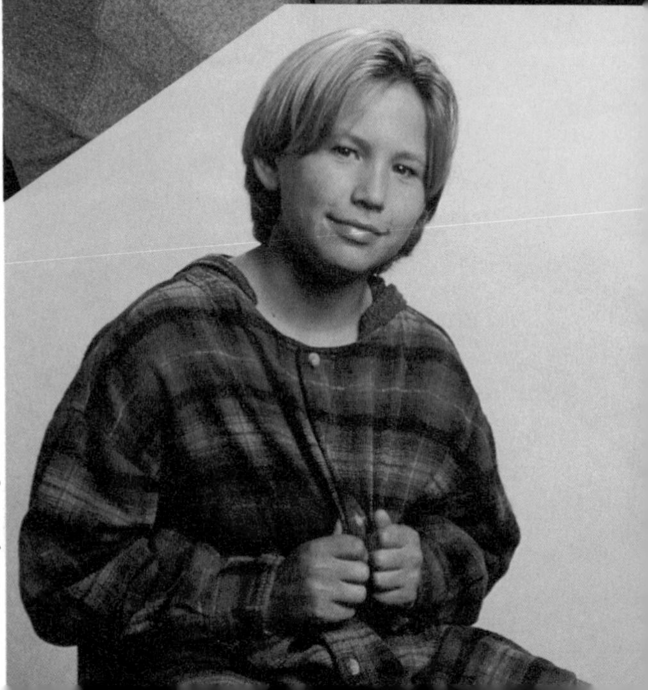

The "mane" event!

friends, do some fishing, hopefully do some traveling."

Actually the possibility of a film for the summer was pretty good. During the past several seasons, movie scripts had been sent JTT's way, but aside from *The Lion King,* he hadn't been able to accept any others because of the timing involved.

However, at this point there were two movies on top of the pile—each was possible, each was *his* for the asking. Jonathan had gotten so popular, he didn't even have to audition.

One of the movies was *Little Giants.* It was the comedic tale of a small Ohio town's Pop Warner football league. Jonathan was interested in *Little Giants* for several reasons: it was a Steven Spielberg Amblin Entertainment production and was being filmed in Los Angeles. He would be able to stay at home and work if he signed on for this flick. The downside was that the film had an ensemble cast and the role he was up for—Nubie, the Giants' gridiron whiz kid and assistant coach—was fairly small. Jonathan turned down the role, and it eventually went to Matthew McCurley, who costarred in *North.* Now, the other movie on JTT's plate, that was something else. . . .

It was a Disney production—a feature film then called *Man-2-Man.* It was to star Chevy Chase and Farrah Fawcett, and Jonathan was up for the role of Farrah's son, Ben.

Though the timing was perfect to do during summer hiatus, *Man-2-Man* was scheduled to film in Vancouver, Canada, which meant that Jonathan would have to spend the summer away from home. If he accepted the role, it would affect not only Jonathan but also his family.

Still, when Jonathan looked over the script, he couldn't help feeling this was the one to do. Chevy Chase and Farrah Fawcett were big stars and the script was good. "There's a lot of laughs, but there are a lot of dramatic, real-life issues, too," Jonathan revealed to the L.A. *Daily News* when asked why he picked this film over *Little Giants*. "It'll make you laugh, and hopefully it'll make you cry."

Once the decision was made, Jonathan really got excited. He had never been to Vancouver but heard it was beautiful. And, as an extra added attraction, there was great fishing up there!

Shortly after *Home Improvement* ended its 1993–94 season, Jonathan and Claudine headed up to Vancouver. He immediately hit it off with Chevy Chase and the rest of the cast and crew. As usual, everyone was amazed at how professional this twelve-year-old actor was.

The director, James Orr, raved to a reporter from the *Los Angeles Times,* "[Jonathan] radiates this intelligence and dimension, and not only does he have this great comic timing but he has this depth of emotions. He's comfortable in his own skin."

In the film's official production notes, Orr stated, "I wanted a young actor who had the soul of a poet, because everything Ben does comes from vulnerability, fear, and insecurity, not from any meanness or inherent negative qualities. Jonathan is very three-dimensional. He's an extraordinary person and very talented. I've rarely met a twelve-year-old who impresses me as much as he does."

During the production, the name of the film changed a number of times. At one point it was *Man-2-Man,* then (as related in *Disney Adventures* magazine) *Pals Forever,* then *Hit the Road Jack,* and eventually *Man of the House.* But one thing that didn't change was Jonathan's enthusiasm and comfortable adaptability as Ben. "I kept waiting to see the flaw," director Orr said of Jonathan's interpretation of his character. "I kept looking for it, and I swear I couldn't find it in ten weeks of shooting."

Jonathan seemed to immediately understand and know who Ben was and what this eleven-year-old was going through. Ben lives with his mom, Sandy (Farrah Fawcett); his dad had left them and run off with another woman. At first Ben was sad and upset by his dad's abandonment, but after five years of being the "man of the house," he had actually grown to like it. Then Sandy's new boyfriend, Jack (Chevy Chase), arrived on the scene with the intention of marrying her. That threatened Ben's position in the family. Jack, who was an attorney, had no idea of what it meant to be a father—or even a stepfather. When it became obvious that his mom was serious about Jack, Ben had to fly into action to drive him away. But no matter what Ben put Jack through, Jack was determined to get the youngster to like him. When Ben suggested Jack join him in the YMCA Indian Guides program and participate in a camp-out and games weekend, it seemed things might be working out. In reality, it was a plot

77

hatched by Ben and his friend Monroe to humiliate Jack and make him look pathetic in the eyes of Sandy. However, in a twist of fate, man and boy were thrown together to fight a mutual enemy when mobsters invaded the camp-out to get Jack for real. Ben and Jack learned a valuable lesson and found out they had more in common than just loving Sandy.

Jonathan's initial take on Ben was right on the mark. In an interview with *Teen Beat* magazine, Jonathan explained his character. "Ben's parents separated when he was very little. So, as Ben, I'm very protective of my mother. I don't really know [Jack] well, so in the beginning I really don't like him. It's not so much I don't like him—it's just that I don't know what he's about. I don't have a clue about who this guy really is. And when he moves in with us, I just draw the line right there. I feel he's totally taking over. I figure I've got to act fast. I see [Jack] is a sort of ick! He's a district attorney, he's got allergies, he's basically a wimpy guy.... I figure if I can get him out in the wilderness, I'll scare him off."

Actually, Ben wasn't so alien to Jonathan's real life. After JTT's parents split up, although he didn't have to be the "man of the house" because of older brother, Joel, he could relate to Ben's predicament. Jonathan discussed Ben's motivation with a reporter from the L.A. *Daily News*. "It's not him being a bad kid," JTT explained. "He's protecting the most important thing in his life. Everything he does is out of vulnerability." And in an even closer-to-home interview with *Kidsday*, Jonathan confided, "Ben came from a single-parent home and I grew up in a single-parent home. I think that in itself was dramatic. Kids have to take on a whole new role, and parents have to do a lot more also. But I think everyone has had their feelings hurt deeply at some point in their lives."

Making *Man of the House* was quite different from Jonathan's *Lion King* work and his *Home Improvement* schedule. Indeed, JTT's whole life changed. He and his mom "lived" in a Vancouver hotel for the ten-week shoot. They had a six-day-a-week schedule and put in nine and a half hours of work a day. Since *Man of the House* filmed between June and August, it overlapped some of Jonathan's regular school year, so once again he had to work with a set tutor. For the camping and games sequences, the cast had to do a lot of preparation. They had to learn an authentic Indian rain dance and how to shoot a bow and arrow. Jonathan even had to take lessons on how to flip a tomahawk. He was pretty good in the end, but he did admit that while he was learning, "The crew had to duck a few times."

It wasn't all problematic, though. As a matter of fact, Jonathan had a lot of fun, especially with Chevy Chase. When they first met, Jonathan was amazed. He turned to his mom and said, "He's huge! Six feet six!" Once Jonathan got over the height factor, he really warmed up to Chevy and announced to friends and family, "He's very nice, very funny. He's kind of flip the way comedians are—I know how to deal with them!"

It was obvious Jonathan had made new friends.

He couldn't stop talking about Chevy. On the *Regis and Kathy Lee* show, he said, "He's hilarious, especially with the physical stuff. He's quick like Tim Allen. I haven't stopped laughing all summer."

And then there was Farrah. Jonathan fell under her spell, too, and enthused in an interview with *USA Today,* "She was great, professional, one of the nicest people to work with. My mom told me what a huge celebrity she was." In *Kidsday,* he added to his praises, "Chevy was a cool guy. He is a veteran actor and getting to work with him was a good thing. Both he and Farrah were good to me. Just being around them and getting to work with two talented actors was cool."

Another way cool aspect of *Man of the House* was filming the "Bee Scene." In this scene Jonathan was required to carry a beehive with ten thousand live bees inside. "They were all over my hands, in my ears, on my nose," he told *Disney Adventures* magazine. "I wasn't scared. I met with the world's foremost bee expert before I did it. He told me everything I needed to know, so I was comfortable going into it. Ten thousand bees, and I didn't get stung one time!"

Though Jonathan spent most of his days during his "summer vacation" working on *Man of the House,* he did get a chance to enjoy the natural beauty and environment of Vancouver. Every chance he got, Jonathan went fishing. "The movie crew flew us over to Vancouver Island to go fishing," he recalled. "We went salmon fishing five times. I caught fifteen fish—but I tried to throw them back, if possible."

So it wasn't all work and no play—indeed, Jonathan always found time to play soccer, even joining some Vancouver kids at their school for a quick kick-'em-up. JTT also made good friends with the rest of the cast, especially Nicholas Garrett, who played his buddy Monroe.

After director Orr called "Cut and wrap" on the final day of shooting, Jonathan returned to his normal routine in Los Angeles. He enjoyed the last days of his summer hiatus and then went back to work on *Home Improvement.* It wasn't until the next spring, March 3, 1995 to be exact, that *Man of the House* hit the movie theaters. March 3 was also the day *The Lion King* video was released—so Jonathan made all sorts of headlines. The funny thing is that Jonathan didn't expect *Man of the House* to be a major box-office hit, so he was incredibly surprised when it was the top grosser of all films the first week it was out. The following weeks, *Man of the House* maintained a steady pace and was quickly considered a hit. It eventually earned close to $40 million.

"I was very surprised that the film came in number one," Jonathan told veteran Hollywood gossip columnist Marilyn Beck. "When I did *Lion King,* I had some idea it would be successful because of Disney's long-term success with animated pictures. But this movie was a shot in the dark."

Jonathan was also surprised that when Disney began the advertising campaign for *Man of the House,* he was the central focus. The posters featured a huge JTT sitting in a chair, dangling Chevy Chase from strings like a puppet—which made it clear that

Jonathan, not Chevy, was the star of the film. And though the reviews for the film were somewhat mixed, there was one unanimous observation: Jonathan Taylor Thomas was an actor to watch!

One reviewer (*Variety*) wrote: "Thomas appears destined for better things, and Disney should corner a share of the youth market with this inoffensive, if seldom funny comedy." *Entertainment Weekly* observed: "Who gets the credit for *Man of the House*'s posting a solid 9.5 million to become the weekend's first place finisher? As with the stepfather/son relationship in the film, the edge goes to Jonathan Taylor Thomas. Following the lead of his *Home Improvement* dad, Tim Allen, Thomas could parlay his sitcom role into a big screen career." The *New York Post* agreed that JTT found the heart of his character. "Jonathan Taylor Thomas makes an effective foil, taking his scheming kid character right up to the edge of the obnoxiousness without altogether sacrificing the affection of the audience." *Daily Variety* commented: "Jonathan Taylor Thomas was the 'man' of the box office as Disney's *Man of the House* led the weekend with an estimated $9.2 million. Chevy Chase and Farrah Fawcett may be *back* in the *Man of the House,* but it's the young *Home Improvement* costar who's receiving credit for the comedy's opening momentum."

And the *Hollywood Reporter* stated: "The surprising strength in *House* comes from the teenage corner. What is essentially a family film that has Chase trying to bond with his girlfriend's son, played by Thomas, has somehow caught the fancy of fickle teens, who normally would not be caught dead at something their younger brothers or sisters might want to see. The probable catalyst is Thomas, who is a bit young to be accorded full-blown heartthrob status but whose TV series is the No. 1 show among adolescents. Whatever their motivation, these most frequent of filmgoers can make or break a movie."

There it was—in black and white—the official acknowledgment that JTT was a major Hollywood power to reckon with!

WE'RE NUMBER ONE!

The *Home Improvement* cast entered their fourth
season in the fall of 1994 in high gear. When they
had said their good-byes for the summer hiatus,
Home Improvement had been rated the number one
prime-time series and had racked up a Golden Globe
award for Tim, an Emmy nomination for Patricia,
and a People's Choice Award for the show itself.
America wasn't the only place that was on a *Home
Improvement* kick—the show was also number one
in Canada and Australia. Tim spent his summer making *The Santa Clause* and writing a book, *Don't Stand
Too Close to a Naked Man,* both of which attracted
huge audiences.

That September Jonathan was on top, too. In previous seasons, to most of the adult TV-viewing audience Zach, Taran, and Jonathan were seen as an
indistinguishable group, lumped together as an unit.
No one had been singled out until Jonathan became

the voice of young Simba in *The Lion King*. Things changed drastically after that. In reviews of *Home Improvement*, JTT was suddenly being referred to as the "number one son." In an article on the series, the trade publication *Variety* discussed the popularity of *Home Improvement* and stated that its cast was especially talented, "particularly Jonathan Taylor Thomas as the middle son—[he's] capable of generating laughs."

Because of *The Lion King*, Jonathan was sought after for many magazine and TV interviews. He was profiled in national publications such as *People, US, Entertainment Weekly,* and *USA Today,* plus the prestigious L.A. *Times* and L.A. *Daily News.* The Hollywood publicity machine was running at top speed. Jonathan was in demand, second only to Tim Allen, on *Home Improvement.* While flattered, Jonathan was not yet wise enough in the politics of show-biz to understand that this might change things. Since he wasn't envious by nature, he didn't realize that others might resent his success. So he went back to *Home Improvement* assuming that he was still close friends with Zach and Taran, ready to resume life on the set as it had been before.

That was not to be. The first signs of Jonathan "pulling away from the pack" was the amount of fan mail he started getting. It was piling up fast, at a rate of more than double of his TV brothers.

Not only was Jonathan feeling the spotlight as the top kid on the show but there was more stress and strain. Going into its fourth season as TV's number one family comedy was a mixed blessing. Of course, it was a thrill to be recognized as America's top show, but it also put the pressure on to maintain those stellar ratings and the quality of the show. Young as Jonathan was, that pressure didn't escape him. He was ever the team player, trying to put *Home Improvement* first.

"It's harder in a sense now that we are in the number one position in the ratings, there's some pressure [and] you're going. 'Oh, man, I want to make the show good,' " explained JTT. "We need to maintain that number one spot, and we need to be the best we can be. We have a responsibility to the viewers to keep up the quality so people will want to continue to watch. We take that responsibility very seriously."

It also didn't help that the network added extra pressure by changing *Home Improvement*'s time slot back to Tuesday at 9:00 P.M. from the comfortable Wednesday berth viewers had grown used to. There was also the fact that they were now "thrown" up against NBC's top-ranked rookie show, *Frasier.*

A spin-off from one of TV's all-time top shows, *Cheers, Frasier* followed the move of psychiatrist Dr. Frasier Crane from Boston to Seattle as he tried to reestablish his life after his breakup with his wife, Lilith. It was a classy—and hysterically funny—show. Viewers were now forced to choose between the two hilariously funny and top-rated shows. The competition was dubbed by some as "Tool Time" vs. "Shrink Time." It was obvious that there was going to be some ratings shrinkage for one of the shows, and the

Home Improvement folks were determined it wasn't going to be theirs.

With this challenge in mind, *Home Improvement*'s fourth season was powered with intriguing new situations for the Taylor family and friends. A shakeup at *Tool Time* forced Tim to deal with a new boss; Jill lost her job on the magazine and considered going back to school for an advanced degree; Tim had to face the frightening midlife crisis of turning forty years old; Brad took on a job delivering newspapers and soon found out he couldn't balance the job and schoolwork; Randy's interest in girls grew by leaps and bounds; and little Mark found out his difficulties at school were because he needed glasses.

In interviews about *Home Improvement*, Jonathan was enthusiastic and cheerily talked about more favorite episodes. "The one with the bully in the bowling alley where he gets handcuffed to a video machine" rated highly with him. Candidly, Jonathan also admitted to favorite episodes hitting especially close to home. "One episode dealt with the *height* issue—which I've dealt with in real life. And Randy's first boy-girl dance party, which was funny and interesting dealing with the girl things, but dealing with parents, too."

Clearly, Jonathan still loved being part of the *Home Improvement* family and looked forward to the new season. "Randy isn't a little kid anymore," he told *TV Guide*. "He's growing up and he's the middle child, so he gets attention being a smart aleck. I like making people laugh."

But Jonathan also admitted to some trepidation.

"It's a lot of work and a lot of long hours, but I have a good time," he said when asked what it was like to be on the top-rated TV show. "Seeing people watch and respond—that's why we make the show. For people to enjoy it, to sit down on Tuesday nights at 9:00 P.M. and laugh for twenty-two minutes. It's rewarding."

Before the season got underway, Jonathan was quoted as saying, "I wish they would get my character more into girls, but they've promised they are going to—the producers talked to me about it." And when Jonathan joined the rest of the Disney TV kids for a preseason press conference, he happily announced, "Randy gets a girlfriend. That's pretty cool!"

The high hopes for the fourth season seemed to be coming true. Not only was Randy's character getting into girls, but Jonathan observed, "They are developing *all* the characters [more]."

Once again, the press was ever interested in the behind-the-scenes atmosphere on *Home Improvement,* and a reporter from the L.A. *Times* spent a day on the set. When the attention was turned on Jonathan, the reporter listed his nonstop activity—JTT sang several verses of the Albanian national anthem, grabbed a cable and cracked it like a whip, circled the set at high speed, and then stopped on a dime and hit his marks and delivered his lines perfectly. Clearly Tim's influence—the ability to be a complete cutup one minute and a complete professional the next—was stronger than ever.

During this season there were more and more kids

on the set behind the scenes, too. No, Jill didn't have the baby she had hoped for, but Patricia's real-life three-year-old twin son and daughter were always there, as was Tim's daughter, six-year-old Kady. To the outside observer the *Home Improvement* set was "all in the family."

Another change all three boys looked forward to was their time out during the work day affectionately dubbed "Rec Time."

"One of the greatest difficulties for children who are holding down the job of an actor is normal child development," explained Gayle S. Maffeo, a Disney vice president, to the *Los Angeles Times* when asked about how the *Home Improvement* kids release their energy. "Kids need to play, and we like to deal with kids who behave like kids."

In order to accomplish that and direct their energy in a positive direction, Disney hired Vikki Van Hoosen and her husband, Angel Aguilera, as personal trainers to Jonathan, Zach, and Taran. The husband-and-wife team started their own company, Personal Edge, in 1992 specifically to provide fitness training for Hollywood showbiz kids. The *Home Improvement* kids were among their first clients—today they also work out with the young actors from *Boy Meets World, Baywatch,* and *Fresh Prince of Bel Air.*

The *Home Improvement* "Rec Time" found a new home during the show's fourth season, quite possibly as a result of the boys "walkout" the previous year. Instead of playing basketball at the truck loading zone, Disney built a special fenced-in area that was large enough to play football, soccer, and basketball and provided a game-filled trailer for rainy days. The trailer housed a mini pool table, a Ping-Pong table, a foozball set, and video games. Most often Zach and Taran played video games, while JTT was more interested in challenging Angel to Ping-Pong. And they all played foozball. Over the Rec area gate was a sign: **"Child Actors Break Area. No one over 16 allowed (NO EXCEPTIONS!)"** Well, Vikki and Angel *are* exceptions, but they've been described as "a couple of big kids," so they fit in anyway.

If the boys were in regular school, they would be getting recess and physical education. "We try and combine [both] in one hour," Vikki said when asked about their fitness training program, which also counts for school credit. From aerobics to sports, the trainers helped each kid individually and together. "We try to include as many different activities as possible so the kids see they don't have to do push-ups and sit-ups to get a workout," Vikki explained. "Some kids have [athletic] skills already, others we have to teach. Taran's learned a lot. He really took to tennis. Zach and Jonathan had good skills already in all sports. They were good athletes. Jonathan's excellent at basketball, but it's not his favorite. Soccer is. What's nice about soccer is you can practice by yourself. You don't need a bunch of other people around."

After Vikki and Angel started "playing" with Jonathan, Zach, and Taran, everyone on the set noticed a big difference, especially Disney exec Gayle Maffeo, who set up the program. "The kids would have so much energy, they'd tend to start taking it out on everybody else," she recalled. "Their attentiveness and performance on the set improved a lot after Vikki [and Angel] joined us."

Zach claimed that Vikki and Angel's training "brought up my coordination tremendously." Taran explained that he most improved in his basketball skills because of their efforts. "I remember I couldn't even make it when the hoop was the lowest—my shots were still two feet short of the net," he said. "Now I can keep up with everyone." As for Jonathan, well, he loves Vikki and Angel, and enthused, "They're great people. They're very nice—professionals and excellent at what they do. They teach us how to stay fit, things that you can do if you don't have much time. It's tough to stay fit on our schedule—working, school. They teach things that are simple ways to stay fit—not difficult—so any normal kid can do it. It's very important to stay physically fit because it's the basis for everything else. You have to be physically fit even to act. It may not seem like they tie together, but it really does because you have to be healthy and well to handle this kind of vigorous schedule. They've helped us maintain that balance. We have a blast! We play basketball, soccer, hide-and-go-seek, run laps around the stages—we do everything, condition ourselves, and get all our excess energy out."

And to show off their athletic ability, the *Home Improvement* kids invited the TV show *Extra* to join them for "Rec Time." Typically Jonathan mugged for the cameras, and in his best Arnold Schwarzenegger/*Saturday Night Live* accent, he promised the audience. "Hi *Extra!* I'm going to pump you up!" Then he, Zach, and Taran took the *Extra* crew through their paces with Vikki and Angel.

Of course, it wasn't all playtime on the set. With the new season of *Home Improvement* came a new school year for JTT. As he prepared to enter seventh grade, he assumed he'd be able to resume his "balancing act"—three weeks working with the set tutor and the fourth week of the month back to his regular classroom.

A consistent A student, Jonathan almost always put in more than three hours a day on his schoolwork. "In my family, education comes before [everything else]," JTT explained when he visited the *Regis and Kathy Lee* show. But sometimes it's easier said than done, and the young actor had admitted that the back and forth between reel life and real life isn't always smooth. "Sometimes the transition has been hard," he said, "but we tell the teachers in advance [about my schedule]. There's a lot of communication. We have Fed Ex come every Tuesday and Friday to transfer work back and forth between the tutor and the school."

Of course, school is not only studies but also students, and it was not always easy for Jonathan to maintain steady relationships with his public school buddies. His back-and-forth schedule put pressure on friendships, even though he worked hard at being just one of the guys. It worked out well during his elementary school years, but when Jonathan entered middle school—in Los Angeles that's sixth, seventh, and eighth grades—things changed a bit. It got tougher because there were older kids who surrounded him sometimes, not to bother him but to give him more attention than he felt he wanted in school. Jonathan was never hassled, exactly, he was just not comfortable. As always, he wanted to be treated like a normal kid at school.

Of that transition to middle school, Jonathan told a reporter, "We're in a good school district, and the teachers here in middle school are helpful. In the past, when they didn't cooperate, they didn't give me the work. That can hurt. That can mess you up, because, you know, your grades—that can be your downfall."

Make no mistake, Jonathan *likes* getting A's.

Jonathan has always been a top student, partly because of his innate intelligence, but just as much because of his interest and eagerness to learn about new things and "old" things—his favorite subject is history. "I've always been fascinated with what went around way back then," he's revealed in many interviews. He's also confessed to not liking "the dreaded math," although he is still good at it— "I just don't like it."

It was during middle school that he transferred from public school to a performing arts school that could deal with his work schedule better. Things started falling into a well-oiled routine once again— at least academically; but that wasn't the case with Jonathan's relationships behind the scenes.

When once Jonathan and Zach had spent all their time together, it was obvious as the fourth season got underway that things had decidedly changed.

Where the boys—in particular Jonathan and Zach— were once inseparable, they were now gradually growing apart. Part of it was brought about by the media attention on Jonathan. When reporters and photographers visited the set, they were ostensibly there for *all* the boys, but more and more they were directing their questions and cameras at Jonathan. Sometimes it was so obvious that a sensitive adult intermediary had to step in and gently nudge the press to please include the others. The whole situation made everyone uncomfortable. Zach and Taran are far too professional to say anything publicly negative about JTT, but they wouldn't be human if they didn't feel bad occasionally—and that made Jonathan feel bad, too.

But besides the spotlight being shone on Jonathan, there were other reasons he was pulling away from the "crowd." Normal, growing-up reasons. Jonathan was developing different interests from his TV siblings. "Taran and Zach pretty much hang out together the most," Jonathan admitted during a Disney press conference, "because they have more in common. They're spending more time together."

Though Jonathan credited a busy schedule as part of the reason he and Zach stopped hanging out so much and having sleep-overs at each others' houses, he also maturely understood a fact of life. "People change," he said. "I've never been one to play with video games, but, yeah, toys I did like. But I kind of outgrew that. People are going to change, and they're gonna have their differences, and those differences are gonna be there for a long, long time."

Other differences appeared here and there. "Taran—he's a *Star Trek*-a-holic," said Jonathan, who doesn't share the fascination. And then there was the food difference. Jonathan is a vegetarian and watches what he eats very carefully. Sometimes it would drive him crazy when the others playfully teased him about it. He told a magazine once, "Zach and Taran love meat. They love steak, veal, hamburger. And what they do is, they get it and they'll walk up [to me] and go 'Hey, cool, *rare,* just the way I like it. Look at all that red meat. Mmmm—cow muscle—would you care for some?"

In spite of those growing differences, JTT realized that when you work with someone, you've got to put those differences aside. "It's very tough to have to work with someone, especially in the situation we're in—like nine and a half hours a day. You *can't* dislike them, otherwise you're gonna go crazy. Besides, we *do* get along—and that shows on the show. I think we have very good chemistry on the set, and it's reflected in the outcome of the show."

Still with the pressure and the personal and professional changes swirling all around him, Jonathan attempted to keep things as normal as possible. However, Jonathan admitted in a recent newspaper interview, "I've had to give up certain things."

CAN YOU FEEL
THE LOVE?

By the tender age of thirteen, Jonathan Taylor Thomas had become a marketable "name" in Hollywood. Link him with a TV show or special, a movie or an event, and a major hit and payday can be predicted. But hand in hand with that kind of power and pull, JTT has always felt a certain responsibility. He loves the attention and love from his fans, but he also feels that he *must* give something back. Even before his popularity crowned him the top teen actor, Jonathan was continually and quietly doing charity work. Jonathan probably does more for a myriad of causes than most other celebrities—of any age.

"My mom has brought me up to be aware of how fortunate I am," Jonathan has repeated when asked why he has gotten so involved in charity work. "She worked with the handicapped and mentally disabled people for fifteen years—in New York and all over the place. She brought me up just to care."

With roots like that, it isn't surprising that Jonathan is so generous with his time and concern. As a matter of fact, Jonathan gets so many requests for appearances on behalf of various charities, he could practically be at one or another every single free weekend—sometimes it seems as if that's exactly what he does.

"There are a lot of different charities—I'll do anything I can do," JTT told a journalist during an interview. And if the charity deals with children, it is even more appealing to him. One of the most impressive aspects of Jonathan's charity work is that much of it is done behind the scenes, out of the press spotlight. He's not in it for the publicity it can get him. Indeed, the only ulterior motive Jonathan has when he helps others seems to be summed up in one sentence, "It makes you count your blessings."

One of the first areas Jonathan has always been concerned with is the environment. He has participated in several "Save the Earth" events, and in 1993 he made a video with three dozen other teen actors for Earth Day. Because of his love of nature, Jonathan admits his perception of the danger the earth faces due to pollution is only heightened when he goes on fishing trips and sees formerly pristine lakes and ocean areas clogged with debris. One of the most memorable moments of Jonathan's outdoors enjoyment was the time he was on vacation in Alaska and saw endangered bald eagles in their natural habitat. In a desire to help animals and protect the ones who face extinction, Jonathan has been finding out more about the organization PETA (People for the Ethical Treatment of Animals).

However, Jonathan's heart, first and foremost, goes out to other children. Besides participating in fund-raisers for organizations such as Michael Jackson's "Heal the World" foundation, Jonathan takes it one step further. For example, when he was asked to make an appearance for the opening for FAO Schwarz toy store in California, he asked the store *not* to compensate him for his time, but to make a two-thousand-dollar donation to charity. And in the same vein, Jonathan had his fee for *The Lion King* book donated to a charity for children. In the past several years Jonathan has lent his name and participated in a number of charitable events, such as appearing in California's Tournament of Roses Parade to benefit the Children's Miracle Network, being named the spokesman for "Kids Helping Kids," and working with the 1993 Athletes and Entertainers for Kids golf tournament, which raised money for various children's charities. He introduced the "Circle of Life" parade at Disney World's Magic Kingdom during the 1995 Cerebral Palsy telethon.

Another program near and dear to Jonathan's heart is Nickelodeon's The Big Help-A-Thon. In 1994 that children's TV network sponsored the first weekend-long telethon to encourage everyday kids to volunteer in their own communities and lend a hand to those in need. "Kids really have a big appetite for making a difference," explained Nickelodeon vice president Albie Hecht about the program.

"They just don't know how to channel their energies for helping. We want to help."

To kick off The Big Help-A-Thon, Jonathan joined such superstars as Whoopi Goldberg and San Antonio Spurs basketball great David Robinson as national spokespeople for the campaign. Jonathan did many radio and press interviews on behalf of the telethon, and on Sunday October 2, 1994, Jonathan spent an exhausting ten hours cohosting it with Nickelodeon's Mark (*Double Dare* and *What Would You Do?*) Summers. Along with celebrity guests such as actress Marlee Matlin, comedian Mark Curry, *Beverly Hills, 90210*'s Gabrielle Carteris, and *Boy Meets World*'s Ben Savage, Jonathan answered phones taking pledges for community service from the viewers. Some of the organizations that became involved were Youth Service America, Earth Force, Points of Light Foundation, Youth Power, National 4-H, and Second Harvest. All these volunteer organizations offered suggestions to kids for their charitable activities.

"The idea is that you don't have to be a celebrity, everyone can give and everyone can help," is how Jonathan explained The Big Help-A-Thon. The message definitely got across because at the end of the telethon thirty-one million volunteer hours were pledged by 4.6 million young viewers. The kids came up with 365 different ways to volunteer their time and help, but Jonathan was most proud that the *idea* caught on. As one little nine-year-old girl volunteer summed it up, "If nobody did anything, nothing in the world would be different. Not everyone realizes that kids can make a difference, too. Some adults think we can't, but we *can*." JTT couldn't have said it better.

Another charity important to Jonathan is the Ronald McDonald House. He first became interested in their work when he was in Portland, Oregon, for a promotional appearance at a local TV station for *Home Improvement*. Whenever Jonathan travels, he tries to find opportunities to visit sick kids; he knows what a special treat it is for them when a celebrity shows he cares. This time he found out about the Ronald McDonald House in Portland.

When Jonathan stopped by the house, all the kids were surprised at how different he looked in person than on TV. They also were impressed at how warm and generous he was. But Jonathan didn't think he was doing anything *really* special—he just wanted to spend some time with the kids and pick up the spirits of those who were facing serious health problems. The Ronald McDonald House is a temporary home for premature babies and children nineteen and under, who are undergoing treatment for a lot of different illnesses, including cancer, kidney transplants, and heart transplants. Many of these kids are critically ill, and all of them are very, very sick, but at Ronald McDonald House they can live in a homelike atmosphere with their parents and family and receive the best medical care available all for free or minimal contributions.

Lorie Wirth, the Housing Program Administrator of Portland's Ronald McDonald House, recalled Jonathan's visit as memorable because he "touched the hearts of the children—and he was touched." Jonathan spent more than an hour talking and visiting with the kids, signing autographs and encouraging the kids in their battle against disease. The adults there all remarked how aware and astute JTT was and how he really left a lasting impression. But Jonathan's concern didn't end with the visit. Afterward he followed up by sending the kids photos that were taken at the time and a beautiful letter telling them how much he enjoyed meeting them. The kids framed the letter and hung it in a place of honor in the teen room.

Jonathan has a strong desire to help kids who aren't as fortunate as he is—especially if they are sick. And, for two years in a row—1994 and 1995—he and his *Home Improvement* brothers, Zach and Taran, have participated in a fashion show and luncheon to benefit Phoenix Children's Hospital's Emily Anderson Family Learning Center. Named for Emily Anderson, a seven-year-old girl who lost her battle with leukemia in 1986, the center is an information and training source for families of ill or injured children. Services include teaching parents how to help their seriously ill children at home, an information resource on children's illness, parenting, and many other related issues. The May 1995 fund-raiser was the fifth annual benefit for the center and during their stay in Phoenix, Jonathan, Taran, and Zach visited kids in the hospital and joined local volunteer kids called the Kids Who Care Gang in a fashion show of Phoenix Suns sportswear. Jonathan wholeheartedly agreed with Taran, who told a Phoenix newspaper reporter, "It's important to give back. Everyone has to deal with illness at some time in their life. We just want to tell the children we understand what they are going through and hope we can make their day a little happier."

With the $80,000 raised at the fashion show, a lot can be accomplished to fulfill the *Home Improvement* brothers' hopes.

Yet another charity Jonathan loves hooking up with is the annual Sail with the Stars Cruise. Every year some of the top celebrity kid stars and their families sail the high seas—not only for their own enjoyment but to help a very important charity. The first year JTT went, it was on behalf of the Juvenile Diabetes Foundation. Paying guests have the opportunity to spend a full week mingling, participating in activities, and getting to know some of their favorite stars like JTT. A major portion of the fees for the cruise goes to the Juvenile Diabetes Foundation.

Jonathan went on his first cruise in 1993. Even his brother, Joel, got in on the action and served as an on-the-scene reporter/photographer for the cruise for *16* magazine. As he snapped photos of Jonathan with fellow stars *Full House*'s Jodie Sweetin and Andrea Barber, *Fresh Prince*'s Tatyana M. Ali, as well as the fans on the cruise, Joel was really impressed with how much time the celebrity kids spent "working." Of course, it wasn't all work—there was a lot of time to play, and after the cruise Joel wrote in his article for *16:* "My brother Jonathan got into all kinds of 'trouble.' In the week at sea, he landed himself in a 'White Cloud'—that's a game where everyone brings a role of toilet paper from their cabin for a celebrity mummywrap contest! He also 'wigged out' at a costume party in full hippie attire, greased it up with Andrea Barber at a '50s party and manned the ship with the captain!"

The following year Jonathan couldn't make the cruise because he was filming *Man of the House,* but nothing kept him away from participating in 1995, this time to benefit the Tubular Sclerosis Foundation. At the height of his popularity, Jonathan found time once more for this love cruise. In between *Tom and Huck* and *Pinocchio,* JTT flew down to San Juan, Puerto Rico, with his mom, brother, several cousins, and his grandfather to board the cruise ship. But this time Jonathan was the *absolute* superstar among the honored guests, which included Jodie Sweetin, Andrew Keegan of *Thunder Alley,* and Will Horneff of the movie *Born to be Wild.* Once again Jonathan participated in the fun and games, but this time he had to have more security. He even had a guard stationed outside his cabin to fend off overanxious intruders.

Still another special cause for Jonathan is Famous Fone Friends. Founded by a group of teachers who tutor celebrity kids on TV and movie sets, Famous Fone Friends began in 1986. The celebrity volunteers call children who are hospitalized or homebound because of a serious illness. They chat about hobbies, school, friends—whatever any friends would talk about on the phone. They also offer emotional support and encouragement to the children who are ill. In the beginning, only three Los Angeles hospitals participated in this program, but today more than two hundred hospitals across the country are connected to this "party line."

Some of the stars who have participated in Famous Fone Friends are John Stamos, Fred and Ben Savage, Jaleel White, Jenna von Oy, Jodie Sweetin, Scott Weinger, Kellie Martin, Jonathan Brandis, Will Smith, and, of course, Jonathan Taylor Thomas.

"Sometimes little kids want to get phone calls from Simba, so I'll do that," explained Jonathan of his work with Famous Fone Friends. Other times he just calls and talks and talks and talks about anything his phone pal wants to. Besides the calls, Jonathan also sends his chat mates things like *Home Improvement* scripts, Simba lion dolls, and all sorts of souvenirs. One little ten-year-old boy who received a phone call from Jonathan enthused, "He was like a regular, nice guy!"

That's just what JTT is—a nice guy. That's how he got involved with doing some charity work for the Boy Scouts of America. While on an appearance for a local ABC affiliate in Cincinnati, Ohio, Jonathan was visiting the station. At the same time the local Boy Scouts were having a Family Jamboree, which was also sponsored by the TV station, so Jonathan took the time out to add something to their festivities. He recorded a public service announcement on bike safety in conjunction with the Boy Scouts of America.

"I feel really grateful that I'm in the position where I'm around people enough and in the public eye enough to have people looking up to me," Jonathan answered when asked why he gets involved with so many charities. "I just think it's real important to be a good and positive role model for all the kids. I just try to be on my best behavior and try to do all the right things."

And when he has had the opportunity to relate one-on-one with his fans, Jonathan never misses a chance to promote these positive messages. "I encourage kids to stay off drugs, stay in school, to make this whole country a better place to live, and hopefully our grandkids and great-grandkids can live in a safer and better environment than we do today."

The funny thing is that Jonathan hasn't only influenced kids to pitch in and help others—he's also set a standard for his *Home Improvement* costars. His attitude is deeply felt on the set, where the entire cast and crew of the show give to charitable causes as a single unit. For example, the show awarded former President Jimmy Carter (who has been a guest star on the series) a check for $100,000 for Habitat for Humanity. That's a charity started by Jimmy Carter and his wife, Roslyn, that builds houses for the needy. The *Home Improvement* check will go toward the construction of two houses.

When Jonathan was discussing his desire to help others with a reporter at a press event, he summed it up wisely, "I value all the charity work, but the best part is inspiring others to do good and feel better about themselves."

Sentiments like this prove that, maybe more than anything else, JTT is a kid who cares!

JTT CONFIDENTIAL
WHAT HE DOES FOR FUN!

Much as JTT loves spreading happiness and enjoyment, he couldn't be as successful as he is if he weren't happy himself. Sure, acting and doing charitable works fulfill him, but he's hardly an "all work and no play" kind of boy.

At home Jonathan is like any other young teen. That's where he can really be himself. One of his favorite pastimes is working *and* playing with his computer. A prized possession of Jonathan's is the CD-ROM game *Wolfenstein*. "It's like you're a soldier in World War II and you're fighting the Nazis," JTT explained to a reporter from *People* magazine. You can also find in Jonathan's computer corner lots of educational CD-ROM software such as a geography program that breaks down the top cities in the U.S.—"It searches your priorities like a low crime rate and great schools and prints out a list," he said.

And then there's *Encarta*, which is "an encyclopedia on CD-ROM. I use it when I'm writing reports."

Of course, when Jonathan really needs a little one-on-one help with his schoolwork, he turns to big brother Joel. "Joel's really, *really* smart, not a nerd though," Jonathan said in a Q-and-A with *Disney Adventures* magazine. "He's always writing these lab reports for honors biology and I have no clue what he's saying."

But once the homework is done, both Jonathan and Joel head outside for a little hoop time. "He's an incredible basketball player," said Jonathan of Joel. "Sometimes we'll play a game of basketball and he kills me. He just dunks over me every time."

Jonathan's life at home is far from the Hollywood scene—there are no *stars* there. That means that both Joel and Jonathan have their assigned chores to do every week. Jonathan takes care of the cat litter boxes, keeps his room neat and in order, and cleans the backyard garden and pool. "There are snails in the backyard and they're always eating our plants—sometimes they fall in the pool," Jonathan said. "I get the wonderful job of cleaning the pool and vacuuming it and getting the snails out—someone's gotta do it!"

Another job Jonathan has is helping plan dinners. Since he's a vegetarian, it's usually pretty simple fare like soup, vegetables, salads, and pasta like macaroni and cheese. Of course, Jonathan is the first to say he *doesn't* actually cook because "nobody would eat it if I did!"

Obviously Jonathan has a full day of work, school,

and chores, but that doesn't mean he goes to bed early. No way. He likes to stay up late. "[I'm a] night person," says Jonathan, who likes to watch C-SPAN on TV before he goes to sleep. "I gotta keep up on daily events," he explains. He also likes to read in bed, and when he can, he stays up to the wee hours just to finish a book.

When asked by *Kidsday* what kinds of books he favors, Jonathan revealed, "I read a book I like several years ago called *The Hatchet* by Gary Paulsen, who also wrote *The River*. He writes about living in the country and surviving. I also like war stories. I've read *The Upstairs Room* by Joanna Reiss. Art Spiegelman also writes interesting books. His dad was in a concentration camp. Art recorded his story, and he expressed his dad's feeling very well in books he writes."

When it finally time for Jonathan to go to sleep, he often has company, his dog Mac. "Mac's a short guy—he just thinks he's a big German shepherd," describes JTT. "He's real ornery, but he's a great dog." So great that Jonathan puts up with his strange sleep habits! "Mac sleeps at the foot of my bed and at night, I don't know why—maybe his mouth is dry—he smacks [his lips]. He has plenty of water down in the bowl, but he just goes like this [Jonathan makes smacking noises] the whole night."

One person who appreciates hanging out with Jonathan in his room and talking fishing is his friend Scott Morrison. He and JTT have been buddies since they met in the fifth grade. "He's just a very cool guy," Jonathan told *Big Bopper* magazine about

Scott. "He's really nice, and he's easy to get along with, and he's very funny."

The two were almost inseparable from the moment they met, but in 1993 Scott and his family moved from Los Angeles to Toronto. Obviously that's made it difficult for them to get together often, but they still manage trips back and forth several times a year. Distance hasn't taken a toll on their friendship, and Jonathan explains, "My best friend is like the same—I don't have a new best friend for every week."

As for Jonathan's Los Angeles friends, he likes to keep his personal relationships away from the show business side of his life. "I figure, in the little free time that I have, if I'm going to hang out with a friend, I don't want to have it industry involved, because that's [already] 99.9 percent of my life," Jonathan confessed to a friendly reporter. "I don't want to talk about showbiz."

One thing Jonathan does like to talk about is SPORTS. But more than talk about sports, he loves to participate! Jonathan isn't shy about admitting he has a competitive nature—"Everyone who plays sports has to have one"—and that's one reason he likes to play team sports. Unfortunately, with his busy schedule today, he's no longer on a soccer team, but he makes up for it by playing basketball and roller hockey whenever he can. Another sport he's becoming quite adept at is snow skiing, which he first attempted while on a vacation with his family.

Of course, Jonathan remains an avid fisherman. It's been his all-time favorite sport since he was first introduced to it when he was five years old and he and his dad would fish the lakes and streams near their home. Since then Jonathan has tried to fish everywhere he travels. "I crave fishing," he says when asked about the sport.

Jonathan admits that he's a bit superstitious about his fishing gear and even has a lucky fishing rod. But it doesn't stop there. "I have the best luck when I wear this," Jonathan confessed while showing off his favorite fishing hat and vest.

Naturally Jonathan also has some fish tales to tell. There's the one about a trip he took in 1990. "I was fishing down in the Coronado Islands off the coast of San Diego and Mexico," he remembered. "This nice yellowtail came by and thought my bait looked mighty tasty and chomped on it—so I hooked him!

"I got the fish stuffed, which was a big mistake. It was expensive—ten dollars per inch [for a total of $360] I now try to let the fish go."

Even when Jonathan goes on promotional junkets, he brings his fishing gear along because "you never know when you're gonna get the chance to fish!" Lately, though, Jonathan has been trying his hand at something new—fly-fishing. Ever since he saw the movie *A River Runs Through It,* he's been trying to find the perfect river fishing spot.

Jonathan becomes more adamant about the decision he made a long time ago to be a vegetarian. He hasn't eaten red meat since he was four years old. "I don't like the concept of eating dead animals," Jonathan has explained of his choice. "When I sat down and realized what I was eating, what I was putting into my body, realized it wasn't good for me. That's the thing. I didn't feel well when I ate this stuff—I got headaches from it. So I said, 'What am I getting out of this? A little flavor that lasts for a second?' So I just dropped it."

Even though he turns down burgers and steaks and the like, Jonathan has a lot to choose from when it comes to his menu. He likes pasta, Mexican food like quesadilla, beans and rice, hummus and other Mediterranean foods, salads, collard and mustard greens. His favorite dinners consist of boiled artichokes, salads with wild rice, baked potatoes, asparagus, tofu and tempura, and for desert, melons such as honeydew and cantaloupe. And ever the comedian, Jonathan adds, "I'm also an excellent pizza orderer—Domino's Pizza, they love me!"

Important as being a vegetarian is to him, he knows it's not for everyone. "I won't give in to peer pressure from friends," he insisted. "But if they want to go to McDonald's, I'll go, have a milkshake, go to the salad bar. I can live with it. I have no problem with people who eat meat—otherwise, I wouldn't have any friends!"

However, Jonathan would be pleased if he does influence one or two friends by his vegetarian example. "I think kids need to learn how to eat healthier," Jonathan has said.

Another aspect of Jonathan's offscreen life is his love of travel. It's hands down one of his favorite things to do, and because of his celebrity status, he gets to do lots of it. Whenever he makes personal appearances, Jonathan tries to find some historical sight in the area to visit. One of his all-time most memorable trips was in 1994 when he went to Europe for the first time. It was for the black-tie premiere of *The Lion King* in London, and while he was there he toured the city like a regular tourist. Since *Home Improvement* doesn't air in England, Jonathan wasn't recognized, so he got to roam around freely. He even visited a Doc Martens shoe factory to see where his favorite footwear was made.

Another trip he will never forget was when he visited Washington D.C. and the surrounding area. He toured Robert E. Lee's mansion, saw Ford's Theater where President Abraham Lincoln was assassinated, and visited the graves of President John F. Kennedy and Senator Robert Kennedy. But the sight that moved him the most was one of the newest additions to Washington's sightseeing attractions—the Holocaust Museum. "I'd just finished reading three books on it for school and for my own personal interest," Jonathan recalled. "It was a very traumatic period of time, a horrible experience for everyone. I was very moved by these pictures [in the museum] and a lot of real-life footage."

Those who have listened to Jonathan describe this visit to the Holocaust Museum are impressed with his very mature observations and historical knowledge. It's much more than anyone would expect from a teenager. It's obvious from even a short time with Jonathan that he is a caring, sensitive person, who also has a true sense of himself.

It is that understanding of who he is that gives him his special style. He is not a trend-follower, but he has developed his own particular image and approach. As for his clothes, well, Jonathan likes the casual but somewhat conservative look. He'll wear jeans, but not ripped ones. He prefers turtlenecks under plaid flannel shirts to T-shirts, and he loves vests. "I like clothes a lot," Jonathan explained. "I think good attire, dressing cool is very popular. I like dressing up and looking my best. I like shopping for clothes that are real cool and neat looking."

But all this talk about mature and conservative might give someone the wrong idea about JTT. He's all boy and all fun! He even describes himself as "Real curious, fun-loving, and like Simba, always getting into mischief."

Jonathan likes to joke around a lot but never at another's expense—just silly stuff like going around and around in a revolving door two or three times when his mom is waiting for him outside. Or telling a story in a funny accent. Actually, Jonathan is a nonstop talker. He loves telling stories and describing something he's recently seen or read. But it's not all about him. Jonathan also asks a lot of questions because he wants to learn. He's curious about people, places, anything that interests him.

And, of course, there is one thing that's beginning to interest Jonathan quite a bit lately ... girls.

GIRLS! GIRLS! GIRLS!

"Dear Jonathan, I am seriously in love with you . . ."

It's no exaggeration to say that Jonathan has received thousands of letters that begin with those words of devotion. Well, maybe not exactly those words but others that are awfully similar, such as "madly in love," "totally in love," "absolutely in love." The point is JTT is on the receiving end of *tons* of love letters.

While most correspondents have never met Jonathan face-to-face, there is something *about* that face, that voice, that smile, that *heart*, that inspires words of heartfelt love and adoration in his countless fans. Of course, the logical extension of those feelings leads to thoughts about the kind of girl Jonathan could feel the same way about.

In this chapter you'll find out all about JTT's "love history" and just how a fan like you might someday be part of it.

No, Jonathan Doesn't Have a Steady!

When Jonathan reads over his mail, he has found the most-asked question is "Do you have a girl-friend?" The answer is a very simple, No, but there's a little bit more to the answer. Jonathan would very much like to have a girlfriend. It's just that he hasn't met the right person yet. In fact, he hasn't even come close.

The real deal is that at fourteen years old, Jonathan has yet to go on a one-on-one date or have a steady girlfriend. In truth, Jonathan has always been sur-prised that so many girls seem to find him attractive and that so many people want to know all that personal stuff about dating and kissing! When one re-porter asked him if he had experienced his first real-life kiss, Jonathan sheepishly responded, "Ummm . . . no, actually." Of course there's plenty of time!

And then when another reporter for the L.A. *Daily News* brought up his legion of female fans, Jonathan suggested modestly, "I never really ex-pected that. It's not something I even planned for. I guess people are fascinated by people on TV."

Girls He Notices

Still, Jonathan has no hesitation about describing his dream girl. She has to be "someone sweet and nice and fun—and most importantly easy to talk to!" Unlike many boys, looks are not on the top of his priority list. "I'm not so into that," he's confessed. "A girl's *personality* is more important."

Take for example the beautiful girls Jonathan has worked with on *Home Improvement*—Pamela Anderson and Debbe Dunning. His TV brother, Zach, has publicly admired the *Tool Time* girls, but to Jonathan they are just colleagues with whom he likes to work.

And how does JTT handle that awkward moment when he finally sees a girl he would like to meet? Well, he let out the secret to *Teen Beat* magazine and said, "I just walk up and start talking. I just start a conversation." And in another interview, this time with *Big Bopper,* Jonathan revealed that he has a lot of gal pals because "girls are easier to talk to [than guys]. Sometimes they can be more fun, and it's easier to go to a movie and just hang out with a girl than it is with a guy."

Girls Who Would Keep His Interest

Would JTT go for a girl who's ... taller than him? ... wore glasses? ... had braces? ... older than him? ... younger? ... a different race or religion? ... lived far away?

It seems everyone wants to know more details about JTT's type and if he has any preconceived ideas about the kind of girl for him. The answer to the second part of that question is an emphatic **"NO!"** Jonathan would never judge a person—girl or boy—by anything superficial. The answer to the first part is also pretty simple. Jonathan's "type" is a girl with whom he could carry on a conversation, share a laugh, confide in, a girl who is understanding, kind, and who cares as passionately as he does about helping others.

As for Jonathan's other interests such as sports, acting, and being a vegetarian, well, it's not necessary for a girl to share all his views. Even if the thought of baiting a hook with a squiggly worm makes a girl nauseous, Jonathan *wouldn't* hold that against her either! If she loves to be active and have fun, if she would rather go rollerblading than staying in and channel-surf the TV, if she loves to joke around, if she is understanding about all the pressures and time demands Jonathan has, she's definitely his "type."

One of the most important things to Jonathan is that a girl be open to new ideas and eager to learn. But just because he's smart in school doesn't mean his perfect girl has to be the class brainiac! Common sense and the ability to just talk—and listen—is more important. "I do want someone I could carry on a conversation with," Jonathan told *Teen Beat*, "but I'm not looking at her report card.... [I like] girls who are smart, ethical, intelligent, kind, and caring."

Hello, My Name Is Jonathan

And just where does a teen idol meet girls? Well, you can scratch out Hollywood parties and clubs. That's not Jonathan's scene. Actually, he meets girls in all the usual places. First of all, there's school, though it's not as easy for him as his classmates. "I'm only in my regular classroom one week out of every four," he told *All Stars* magazine. "That does allow me to meet people there. Still, it's difficult."

And then there's work. Of course, there are no young actresses who are regulars on *Home Improvement,* but every so often there are guests like Kimberly Cullum, who played Randy's girlfriend. No love match was made there offscreen though! However, the *Home Improvement* set isn't so lonely as you might think. It's right in the middle of the Disney Studios lot, where other shows also tape. And a lot of them do feature younger actresses, such as *Boy Meets World*'s fourteen-year-old Danielle Fishel, who is a casual acquaintance of Jonathan's—nothing more. *Thunder Alley* also taped on the lot—until it was canceled—and JTT did develop more of a friendship with cute costar Kelly Vint, who played Claudine. But no way was it ever a romance.

It also makes sense that Jonathan would meet girls on movie sets, but that wasn't the case on *The Lion King,* where he worked alone, nor on *Man of the House,* where all his fellow Indian Guides were boys. It's safe to say Jonathan won't be meeting that dream girl on the set of his upcoming film, *Pinocchio,* since there are no actresses near his age in the cast. But what about *Tom and Huck,* the movie Jonathan filmed during his 1995 summer hiatus? Well, he did share an on-screen smooch with costar Rachael Leigh Cook—she played Becky—but the two did *not* share any unscripted kisses.

If Jonathan weren't a TV star, he might meet girls in the normal places like malls or friends' houses. But most of the time he's at a mall, it's for a special "Meet & Greet" for an event. He loves doing these because he does get to really meet his fans, but it still doesn't give Jonathan enough time to get to know someone. "We usually have an autograph session of fifteen to twenty minutes," he explains. "I talk to kids, answer their questions, and sign autographs." But he doesn't end up making many lasting relationships there.

Truth is, while there are opportunities to *meet*, establishing and maintaining a relationship—even a friendship—is close to impossible with Jonathan's hectic schedule. JTT accepts this sacrifice—for now. "I think that dating is not an easy thing," he told *16* magazine. "It's the type of thing where you have to be in this group, to go and meet these people. It's difficult when you're on the [*Home Improvement*] set nine and a half hours a day and then going off to make movies and things. It's difficult to keep up with any kind of relationship, even with a friend."

Of course, having a girlfriend is not impossible. "It's just not easy," he continued. "But if you're really into it and committed to this person that you want to go out with, you have to make time."

Does She Like Me for Who—or What— I Am?

A universal problem when it comes to celebrities and relationships is sorting out the reasons why someone might show interest. Jonathan is no exception. He does worry that some girls might like him *just* because he's on TV. "Yes, it's a concern," he confided to a friendly interviewer. "I have to be very choosy about who I surround myself with. I don't want to have anyone around who's just there to say, 'Hey, I know this guy, he's on *Home Improvement*— he's a celebrity.' That's not what I want. I want a girl or any friend, really, to like me for me, not for what I do."

Of course, sometimes it's hard to be able to recognize a girl's motives when Jonathan first meets her. She could be showing interest for all those wrong reasons. But JTT tries to rely on his natural instinct when it comes to meeting new people. "I can read people fairly well," he continued. "I think I'm a good judge of character. I mean, you can't judge a book by its cover, you can't just see the person and decide 'Oh, she's using me.' You have to get to know her first. I think eventually little signs show up. I've been lucky, though. I haven't really had that problem so far."

The Truth About Those Rumors

Since Jonathan is in such a spotlight, he faces that age-old celebrity problem: the rumor mill. Even though he's only fourteen, Jonathan has had rumors spring up about, of all things, his love life! Partly it goes with the territory of being famous. But there's another reason why there's so much speculation about his dating habits. Many fans find it hard to believe that he *doesn't* have a girlfriend. They argue, he's *such* a great catch, it's amazing that no one's hooked him yet!

And so the rumors run rampant. Most have never traveled beyond one or two schoolrooms, but there are four stories in particular that have taken to the information superhighway. First there's the one about JTT and Jodie Sweetin, the young actress who played the middle sister, Stephanie, on *Full House*. It's been reported that they are in Hollywood terms, "an item," that they are going together. This has never been true. Jonathan has met and even spent time with Jodie at some charity functions and Hollywood events in the past. Both Jodie and Jonathan were on the 1993 Sail with the Stars cruise, but so were hundreds of other people. They did not become boyfriend and girlfriend back then—or even really friends. They have never exchanged phone numbers or attempted to keep in touch. That's why the rumor is so surprising to both of them!

The second rumor that's making the circuit is that Jonathan and actress Kimberly Cullum are dating. It's easy to see how this one came about, since Kim, the real-life sister of *Grace Under Fire*'s Caitlin Cullum, did play the girl Randy liked in the party episode of *Home Improvement*'s fourth season. (It was the one where Tim overwaxed the recreation room floor where the kids were dancing.) But that episode was taped in under a week, and JTT and Kimberly's scenes were done in two days. That didn't leave a lot of time for sparks to fly—and they didn't.

Rumor three concerns Jonathan and Rachael Leigh Cook, who played Becky in the film *Tom and Huck*. Once again the "insider reports" were flying fast and furious that an on-set romance at the Alabama location had blossomed between the two. After all, they did share an on-screen kiss. What better way to start a romance? Except in their case it didn't, and once the cameras stopped rolling, Jonathan and Rachael went their separate ways. In fact, Rachael was really on the set only for a week or two—just enough time to shoot her scenes and then fly home.

And finally, the fourth rumor making the rounds is about Jonathan and *Thunder Alley*'s Kelly Vint. This one is a little tougher to refute because there is a glimmer of truth to it. But just a glimmer. You see Kelly, who's now thirteen, first met JTT during "Rec Time" on the Disney lot set. She was playing Claudine Turner, and JTT recognized her from the movie *Stargate*. They realized they had a lot in common and liked each other enough—as friends—to go out. But they went out with a group of kids, never as a twosome. The real scoop is that they went out to the movies twice, and—this is really hard to believe—Kelly called it quits before anything had really begun! When quizzed about her "dates" with JTT, Kelly candidly told a group of reporters, "Yes, I actually went out with Jonathan. I went out with him twice. [But] he's more of a friend to me than a boyfriend. He's very nice. He's very mature. He's very smart. He likes to go out. We went to the movies. We saw *Junior*, and I went to see *My Girl II* with him, and that time he talked all through the movie! I'm sitting there going, ummmm ..."

The Dating Game

Truth is with Jonathan's lifestyle and schedule, there isn't much time for dating right now. "I go to the movies with a group, but no one-on-one dating yet," Jonathan confirmed to the L.A. *Daily News.* "That's not something I really want to do now."

In the same vein, Jonathan told another reporter from the New York *Daily News* that his approach to dating isn't so unusual in the 1990s. "Kids my age don't actually go out on what adults would technically call dates," he explained.

But don't get Jonathan wrong—he's not antisocial; he's not a hermit or loner. He loves to socialize and go out with friends—girls included! Some of the things he enjoys most is playing basketball, football and tennis, or going Rollerblading or to the beach. Of course, there's always fishing!

If Jonathan is out on the town at night, he and his friends usually go to a restaurant first. Preferably it's Mexican, Italian, or one that specializes in health or vegetarian dishes. Next it's usually on to the movies. Not surprisingly Jonathan's movies of choice are comedies like *Forrest Gump,* but he also likes action films if they're not too violent. When he's with friends of his own age, he usually sticks to PG or PG-13 rated films. One thing is for sure, though, Jonathan does *not* like to go see his own movies with his friends. It makes him feel uncomfortable; it's as if he's back at work!

Another way Jonathan likes to spend time on his group dates is at home watching rented videos. Even though he's "in the business," Jonathan doesn't usually have time to catch *all* the films he'd like to see when they first hit the movie theaters, so stopping by a video store and renting one is just up his alley.

And what else does this heartthrob like to do when he goes out? Well, if Boyz II Men are in concert anywhere near Jonathan, he'd like to be there. They are his all-time favorite group, and he knows all their songs by heart. He's yet to attend his first Boyz II Men concert, but he'd like to.

What to Do, What to Say If You Meet JTT

A lot of girls fantasize about meeting Jonathan, and the truth is it's not all that impossible. Even if you don't live in the Los Angles area, you have a chance. Jonathan travels so much doing personal appearances, making movies, doing charity events, he's stacked up frequent flyer miles winging all over the country. It's easier than you think to find out where he's going to be. Read the newspapers and magazines or listen to the radio to see if there are any upcoming visits. Call your local ABC-TV affiliate and find out if they are bringing him to your town for a *Home Improvement* event, as they will be in January 1996 in Harrisburg, Pennsylvania. Check out any local charity events he might be appearing at. He does "Meet & Greets" all the time when he's traveling, and he definitely loves it when fans come up to him and introduce themselves. He's met fans all over the world during these chat stops, and he gets letters and calls from friends he's made in such places as Huntsville and Mooresville, Alabama, Vancouver, Canada, Miami, the Caribbean, Cincinnati, Atlanta, Phoenix, New York, London, England, and Prague.

If you live in or are visiting L.A., you can get free tickets for a taping of *Home Improvement* and Jonathan usually spends time chatting with the audience afterward. If that is out of the question, you can always write Jonathan via his fan club, ABC-TV, or even connect with him on-line through the ABC-TV forum on America Online.

Getting in touch with Jonathan is one thing, but the question is what do you say when you meet him? First and foremost, don't be shy. He doesn't like to be the center of attention and put on the spot, so don't ask a zillion questions about showbiz or tell him how cute he is. Do talk about yourself and tell him about the things you're interested in. If you like sports or fishing or traveling or are involved with charity projects, you definitely will have things in common. Just remember, treat Jonathan just like any other friend, because that's just what he wants to be, your friend!

12

THE UPS AND DOWNS
OF FAME

There's a lot more to being an actor than memorizing scripts and hitting the mark for the camera. It takes dedication, hard work, and a lot of sacrifices. Of course, for some who have chosen acting as a career, stardom is the reward. And while that may sound enviable, it, too, has its ups and downs.

Jonathan may have started out as a child actor, but by the time he reached his teen years, he had become a star. "I never really expected all this; it's not something I ever planned for," JTT admits. Still Jonathan would be the first to agree that there is much he loves about his newly minted status, especially getting to do cool things that most ordinary kids never would—but because he's so honest, he'd also admit that there are times when he wishes he wasn't quite so famous after all.

At first, when the spotlight turns its bold bright attention on an actor, it can be pretty exciting. One of the best perks of glitz and glamour for Jonathan is getting to meet and mix with some of his idols. He's invited to Hollywood premieres and parties all the time and *his* name is on the hottest VIP lists. He's been part of the gala festivities for the openings of Planet Hollywood restaurants in San Diego and Atlanta and even hung out with superstar owners Bruce Willis, Demi Moore, Arnold Schwarzenegger, and Sly Stallone. At the London premiere of *The Lion King,* Jonathan spent some quality time with music megastar Elton John. Even more exciting for sports fan JTT, he thought it was incredibly cool when he met former boxing heavyweight champ Evander Holyfield—who autographed boxing gloves for him—as well as the current champ, George Foreman, who guested on *Home Improvement.*

There were others. "I had a dream come true when I met Dee Brown of the Boston Celtics," Jonathan recalled. "I've been a big fan for a long time, and when he came to Los Angeles to play the Clippers, I even got to go backstage and met the entire team. It was a blast. I got autographs and an NBA ball."

As an all-star kid, Jonathan also gets invited to some of the most fun events around, like Wrestlemania. He got to ride on Disneyland's brand-new Raiders of the Lost Ark ride, not only for free but before it was even open to the general public.

Then, there are the freebies. *Everyone* seems to be handing them out to the young star. Whenever

JTT goes to a Planet Hollywood or Hard Rock Cafe, he comes away with bags full of goodies: T-shirts, caps, jackets. He could actually build an entire wardrobe from the giveaways alone. "I have a huge collection of hats from different companies," JTT has described. The sports and clothing companies like Reebok, Nike, Adidas, J. Crew, and Doc Martens also send Jonathan their newest lines regularly. All they hope is that the much-photographed young star wear their shoes or clothes out in public or in photo shoots. It's good advertising for them.

Another perk of fame is the publicity and attention routinely showered on JTT. Profiled on such TV shows as *Entertainment Tonight, Extra, Regis & Kathie Lee,* and *Good Morning America,* it has given Jonathan the opportunity to talk about his latest projects and even publicize charitable causes that are close to his heart.

Jonathan has also been invited to appear at several glamorous TV award shows. He got to present Elton John and Tim Rice a Golden Globe award for Best Song for *The Lion King*'s "Can You Feel the Love Tonight." He did presenting honors at the SAG Awards ceremony as well, and was front and center at the People's Choice Awards when *Home Improvement* took home the top comedy trophy in 1994.

In addition, Jonathan also hosted TBS-TV's Cybermania '94 Awards show with actor Leslie Nielsen, which was the first televised interactive awards show. Trophies went to the best CD-ROMS and video games of the year. One reason JTT is in demand as a presenter is because he's gotten so famous himself—

another is that he can be counted on to never mispronounce a nominee's name or goof up his speech!

Another obvious perk of being an all-star kid is the money. Let's face it, showbiz sure pays better than a weekend baby-sitting job or clerking at a video store. Most kids with afterschool jobs pull in the minimum wage of around $5.50 per hour; working showbiz kids can expect to earn thousands of dollars per week. Of course, by law most of that money goes into trust funds and savings accounts, but young actors do end up with more pocket money than the average teenager. JTT is no exception, and he absolutely appreciates what those extra dollars can buy. "The best part of being in showbiz is being able to buy stuff I enjoy like fishing equipment and going on fishing trips," he once said.

But Jonathan is hardly a spendthrift—not by a long shot. The fact that he is earning top dollar right now has allowed him to be secure with his future, which is important to anyone who wasn't born with a silver spoon in his mouth. Jonathan appreciates the value of money and the opportunity he's had to earn it. "I save my money," he says. "I think everyone's tempted to spend it, but the right thing to do is save it." And then he adds in typical boy fashion, "Of course, once in a while I'll see something—usually fishing gear or baseball cards—that I've gotta have and I'll go get it."

The most heartwarming part of being famous, however, is the fans. JTT has them by the barrelful. He gets *tons* of fan letters, up to five thousand a week. He's grateful for every single letter—for two reasons. Professionally, getting this much mail tells JTT's bosses just how popular he really is. That's important. With that kind of affirmation, his role on *Home Improvement* has been beefed up considerably, and he's received significantly more movie offers than ever before.

But more importantly, perhaps, is how all that mail makes Jonathan feel. It's incredibly heartwarming. It really makes him feel good that people out there appreciate his work and care about him. It is not something he has ever taken for granted.

Indeed, Jonathan's greatest wish involves his fans and the letters they send him. "If there's one thing I could do besides making a better world, it would be to *write back more,*" he says. "I get swamped with fan letters, and I *do* read them. I appreciate each and every letter. I feel bad that kids take the time and effort to write stuff that comes from deep down in their hearts. It's *real* important stuff. I'd love to sit down and write a two-page letter to each one, and if I had the time, believe me, I would."

Since JTT can't write back to all his fans, he tries to meet as many of them as possible. JTT gets a kick out of the many autograph sessions he has all over the country. And he almost always ends up staying longer than scheduled to make sure *everyone* gets a handshake, an autograph, and often an instant snapshot with him. "I never want to disappoint anyone," is Jonathan's motto.

The Other Side of the Coin

But Jonathan sometimes gets upset that he can't respond to each and every fan personally. Which is part of the *downside* of fame. Sometimes Jonathan just can't be everything to everyone. He's only human ... and he's only fourteen years old! For that reason, fame can also be something of a burden to Jonathan.

His success has brought out the jealousy in some of his peers. After all, other young actors wouldn't be human if they didn't feel some twinges of envy for JTT. Sometimes they forget that it isn't his fault he's so popular.

Only recently Jonathan was invited to play in a sports game with other teen actors. But on the way to the event he got lost and arrived late. Instead of waiting for an explanation, at least one not-so-famous young actor yelled, "Oh, Jonathan *had* to make an entrance—so he purposely came late." JTT was given no chance to explain.

Comments like that really hurt Jonathan's feelings. He wouldn't be human if they didn't. There's jealousy in his private life as well. In an interview with *TV Guide*, JTT recalled how some schoolmates reacted to him when he was first on *Home Improvement.* "The bigger kids like to give us a hard time, trying to put us in the trash cans and stuff." Sounds like a scene from his TV series, but it was really nothing to laugh at!

Neither is the attention Jonathan sometimes gets from the press. His every move and action is dissected and put under the publicity microscope. The first time he felt the sting of media criticism was, of course, during the *Home Improvement* flap when all the boys were slammed for being "greedy" without getting a chance to explain their side of the story. That was a tough lesson in how unfair fame can be at times; but that wasn't the only instance Jonathan was singled out by the "poison pens" of the press. Ironically, he's found himself under fire for just being *himself!* For Jonathan *is* a very intelligent, very well spoken young man. In some press accounts his articulateness has been termed "jarringly erudite," as if he were a phony because he's such an intelligent conversationalist. Instead of being impressed with his maturity and understanding, Jonathan was accused of being "programmed" and having "well-rehearsed answers to questions."

When a kid reporter from *Kidsday* asked Jonathan if the jealousy and criticism he's encountered bothers him, he candidly answered, "I think everyone has had their feelings hurt deeply at some point in their lives." It's safe to say, Jonathan certainly has, too.

Perhaps the biggest sacrifice to stardom is the trade-in of a normal lifestyle. Jonathan's mom told the *National Enquirer,* "I work hard to keep Jonathan a normal kid." But the truth is Jonathan's life is anything but normal compared to that of most fourteen-year-olds. "I've had to give up a lot of things," JTT himself admitted shyly to a journalist. Not the least of which is his beloved soccer. He simply has no time to be at practice or even go to all the games. And JTT deeply misses being part of a team—being just "one of the guys." And then there are his friendships. Many of them have fallen victim to his superstar status. Now Jonathan always has to be on guard when he meets new people. It's always in the back of his mind that new pals may just want to hang out with him and be his friend because he's on TV, not because of his personality.

Add to this mix the pressure of trying to live a normal life, working a steady job, going to school, traveling around the country and the world and it's spelled S-T-R-E-S-S! Jonathan isn't immune to this mostly adult complaint. He's such a sensitive kid, he takes all his responsibilities to heart. He told *People* magazine, "You have school, friends, learning your lines, and making sure your performance is up to speed. I can't tell you how many shows I've done with full-blown migraine headaches."

Truthfully, his kind of go-go schedule can really take its toll. It can lower one's resistance and Jonathan *has* been prone to the flu, stomach viruses, and sore throats. Yet he continues to keep up this breakneck pace. Why? Well, it goes to the heart of who Jonathan Taylor Thomas really is. He's just so very thankful for his success and wants to share that and bring joy to others, but most importantly, JTT *never* wants to disappoint anyone!

TOM AND HUCK

If the fan mail for JTT piles high at *Home Improvement* studios, it's nearly equaled by the tons of movie scripts and offers that arrive daily at his agent's office. Because Jonathan is such a talented and high-profile young star, he's on the "most wanted" list for movies with young protagonists. Happily, JTT loves making movies, and his success now allows him to pick and choose the best ones to be in. In the summer of 1995, the best one offered was a true American classic—*Tom and Huck*.

The movie *Tom and Huck* was the vision of filmmakers Laurence Mark and John Baldecchi, who several years ago had produced *The Adventures of Huck Finn*, which starred Elijah Wood. Ever since then, they'd seen the possibilities of another movie based on the classic Mark Twain book *The Adventures of Tom Sawyer*. By the end of 1994 screenwriters Stephen Sommers, David Loughery, and Ron Koslow had finished a script, and the producers had a go-ahead to make the movie. All they needed was a rough 'n' tumble teen to play the lead character. And there was no question in their minds—they wanted Jonathan Taylor Thomas.

While negotiations were going on between the producers and Jonathan's agents, the young star wanted to tell everyone he was up for this terrific role, but he knew better. Often in showbiz, even when things seem set and ready to go, something unexpected happens and projects fall apart. So Jonathan kept quiet when asked if he had any movie plans for the 1995 summer hiatus from *Home Improvement*. But by the start of the year, the ink was dry on the contracts, and Jonathan's participation was signed, sealed, and delivered. On January 13, 1995, the Hollywood trade papers carried the announcement. The headlines read: "THOMAS SET FOR SAWYER"—and so he was!

Though Jonathan wouldn't arrive on the Huntsville, Alabama, set until the end of April, the filmmakers were working nonstop in preparation. British director Peter Hewitt signed on. Costume and set designers were given the go-ahead to recreate the clothes and atmosphere of the south along the Mississippi River in 1845. And, during this time, the film, which was an independent production, was picked up by Disney to distribute. Even though Jonathan was still busy at work on his TV series, he was called in to help audition young actors and actresses for the important costarring roles of Huck Finn and Becky Thatcher. For Jonathan, all this "prep" time was thrilling, and he told *anyone* who would listen, "I'm very excited about this!" He expanded his thoughts to *16* magazine, saying: "I love the idea! I love great books, I love history and the idea of dressing up in costumes from the 1800s. To me, that's really cool!"

Actually, *Tom and Huck* was the first time that Jonathan was the real, true, headlining star of the film from the very beginning. But that wasn't the *only* reason he wanted to do *Tom and Huck.* "I think it's cool doing a period piece—that's part of the appeal of it you know, the costumes and where we're filming it," he told a reporter. "I think it'll give me a good background of what it was like to live back then, because the director was telling me he wants to make it very authentic—real, like these kids would have acted back then.... [Also] I just thought this was a classic piece—it hasn't been done in a number of years, so why not?"

Although Jonathan had not read the original Mark Twain book at the time, he was totally intrigued by the story when he got hold of the script. He told *Teen Beat* that was one of the deciding factors for him to do the film, "Tom Sawyer is a classic role. It's a role that most Americans are familiar with, and the character, Tom Sawyer, is about as real a boy as you can get. He's precocious, he's always thinking. So I like the character, and I like the actual piece, so I figured why not do it?"

But there was even more to it than that. "Another reason I wanted to do the film," JTT continued telling the magazine when they asked if he was similar to the character of Tom Sawyer is that, "we're not exactly alike. I do have to challenge myself as far as acting. The film takes place in 1845, and during that time Tom Sawyer was atypical. He was rambunctious, and back then, people were very reserved and reformed, and he kind of stuck out like a sore thumb."

But there were some similarities, too, and Jonathan admitted, "Of all the characters I've played, I'm probably the most like Tom Sawyer—adventurous. I don't know if I'm so precocious as Tom Sawyer is; he's pretty conniving. But we're both active and have a sneaky side to us."

Besides the chance to do a role like Tom, Jonathan was intrigued with traveling to a part of the United States he'd never been before. "[I'm looking forward to] being down in Alabama," he said shortly before he left for location shooting. "I like traveling and I've never been to Alabama. Huntsville is in the north, near Tennessee. It's a beautiful state and we'll have a good time."

The Huntsville, Alabama, location was picked to represent the fictional town of St. Petersburg, the setting of the yarn of life along the Mississippi River in the mid-1800s. Based on some real-life childhood adventures of the author Mark Twain, *Tom and Huck* captures the lazy summer days of a southern town along a waterway dotted by riverboats, gamblers, and cutthroats. Tom and his friends Huck and Becky are caught between the rules of the genteel folk of St. Petersburg and their natural rebellious nature. And when they accidentally witness a murder in a graveyard, they promise to keep silent and stay out of trouble. But Tom had a horrible time of living with the guilt, and when an innocent man went on trial for the murder, he finally fingered the culprit, Injun Joe.

But the story doesn't end there. That's only the beginning of the adventure, in which Tom and Huck test their wits and luck as they try to escape the wrath of the ruthless Injun Joe! Along the way Tom and Becky get lost in a cave; Tom and Huck discover a secret treasure and find themselves traveling down the mighty Mississippi on a log raft that eventually crashes into rocks. In the end, they find the *real* treasure—an understanding of friendship and loyalty they never knew before.

Jonathan's preparation for his role began long before he and his mom, Claudine, headed down to Huntsville. First of all there were the wardrobe fittings for the costumes he would wear. After all, *Tom and Huck* takes place in the mid-1800s in St. Petersburg, Missouri, and Tom didn't exactly dress like *Home Improvement*'s Randy Taylor, or JTT at all. No Reebok high-tops and khakis! Instead, Tom wears buckskins, moccasins, and wide-brimmed hats, all of which had to be custom-made for Jonathan and the other young actors in the movie. Jonathan eventually had to cut his long hair for the role. Since there were no designer stylists in the 1800s, Tom wore what was called a "bowl cut." It looked as if someone had put a bowl on his head and cut around the rim. Jonathan had to even darken his blondish hair to brown, so he definitely had a different look!

The actual casting of Huck Finn and Becky

Thatcher was something else JTT was involved in before filming began. Though Jonathan didn't have to audition for *his* role, he did read with a number of the most promising kids up for the roles of his friends. When the audition process ended, the coveted roles went to Brad Renfro as Huck and Rachel Leigh Cook as Becky, choices Jonathan wholeheartedly approved of. Though he didn't know either of them before *Tom and Huck* and hadn't seen Brad in his debut movie, *The Client,* Jonathan was impressed by Brad's tryout.

Of Brad, JTT recalled, "When we read together, I thought he was very talented. He's a really good actor. And hopefully together we can make a real good movie."

Although JTT didn't know it, Brad Renfro has an interesting story. Brad, who turned thirteen after *Tom and Huck* wrapped, was just ten years old when he first performed in front of the cameras. He was anything but a Hollywood kid. When *The Client*'s director, Joel Schumacher, described his requirements for the actor who would play streetwise eleven-year-old Mark Sway in that 1993 movie, a nationwide search began. "I wanted an intelligent kid who's a tough and savvy survivor, a kid with an authentic southern accent, a kid from a trailer park, like the character in the movie," Schumacher told *The New York Times.* "I wanted a kid who understood in the marrow of his psyche what it was like to grow up too soon. Easier said than done."

Until they found Brad Renfro of Knoxville, Tennessee, that is. In something of an unorthodox approach, casting director Mali Finn (who also discovered Edward Furlong (*Terminator 2*) at a California youth center) contacted alternative schools, boys clubs, YMCAs, churches, and even police departments and asked if they knew any tough kids who showed acting ability. "Not that we were looking for a delinquent," explained Finn, "but a tough boy."

A policeman in Knoxville, Tennessee, contacted Finn and told her about a ten-year-old boy who had just played a drug dealer in a school production sponsored by DARE. It was Brad Renfro. Finn, who had met about 5,000 boys and interviewed nearly 1,500 of those, recalls when she met Brad, "He was mesmerizing. From the second he walked in, I had the feeling this was it. I usually taped each applicant for ten or fifteen minutes. I let the tape run an hour with him."

Not only was the casting director impressed with Brad, so was the director. For Brad fit all the requirements, all the way around. Brad was an only child, who's lived with his grandmother since the age of three. His father works in a factory in Knoxville, and his mom had remarried and moved away to Michigan. Brad, young though he was, had definitely known some of life's hard knocks. All that—and more—translated onto the screen.

After earning outstanding reviews for *The Client*, Brad was cast in another big movie, *The Cure*. The director was Peter Horton of TV's *thirtysomething* fame, and the movie would costar Joseph Mazzelo of *Jurassic Park*. The story was about the relationship between two boys, one of whom (Joseph) had been diagnosed with AIDS, the other (Brad) who searched for a cure. Again Brad won rave reviews. But director Horton also remembers something else about working with Brad—the emergence of a young heartthrob. Brad had turned twelve during the filming of *The Cure,* and Horton told the *New York Post,* "He was becoming a movie star with this gaggle of girls, mostly thirteen- to twenty-four-year-olds, who would follow him from location to location."

And then there was Rachael Leigh Cook. This native of Minneapolis, Minnesota, was fifteen when she was cast in the role of Tom Sawyer's young love, Becky Thatcher. That, needless to say, was the most coveted role of all to JTT fans across America. Unlike Brad Renfro, Rachael had always dreamed of a career as an actress. She had started out as a print model for local Minneapolis advertisers, and in 1993 she was cast in a short film called *26 Summer Street.* Her next role was Mary Anne in the summer 1995 feature film, *The Babysitters Club,* but when she found out she was up for Becky in *Tom and Huck,* she admits she was surprised. Rachael just didn't believe she was right for the part. "First of all, I'm fifteen and Becky's like twelve," Rachael, who'd read the book, explained. "She has long blond hair, the whole bit." But she went to the audition, with a professional attitude. "I'm just going to do my darnedest anyway—just do what I can do." Obviously, "what she could" was just what the casting directors were looking for.

Besides being talented and pretty, Rachael had

something else going for her that many of the other actresses who competed for the role of Becky didn't. Rachael is short for her age—just under five feet two inches tall—and Becky had to appear to be smaller than Tom. Most of the actresses who were the right age and look for Becky were taller than Jonathan, who is still growing but during the filming was just hitting the five-foot mark!

Rachael didn't know either Jonathan or Brad before *Tom and Huck*. Of course, she knew *who* JTT was, though she says she doesn't really watch *Home Improvement* often. But when she read with him for the role, Rachael was very impressed with his maturity and professionalism. "He was fun to talk to," she recalled. "Very neat, very intelligent, a good conversationalist. We talked about fishing because he loves it and I've been. I'm from Minnesota, and he wanted to know what life was like there."

Of course, Minnesota was a far cry from the *Tom and Huck* Alabama location sites. The cast and crew stayed in the small city of Huntsville, nestled in the rolling foothills of north central Alabama. Besides its southern charm and historical significance, Huntsville is also home to the high-tech industry of the U.S. space program. The NASA center that built rockets to carry the first Americans into space and is presently developing new rockets for the Space Shuttle program is located in Huntsville. Needless to say, all this history and high-tech stuff was right up Jonathan's alley, and he looked forward to really learning more about it.

In the end, though, there was really very little time

to go space-exploring during the nine-week movie shoot. Instead, Jonathan spent most of his time in the small, secluded hamlet *outside* of Huntsville called Mooresville. When Jonathan first heard about their shooting site, he said, "They found this town, Mooresville—it has like fifty people and it's beautiful. It has a lot of caves, where we're filming, with stalactites and stalagmites."

Even before the cast and crew arrived in Mooreseville, preparations were being made there for *Tom and Huck*. As early as March, a crew was building sets, including a jail, a blacksmith shop, and a barrel maker's shop. They even constructed the house where Tom lived with his Aunt Polly—all with the authentic feel of the 1800s. Luckily, there already were some local buildings with architecture that fit right in. Additionally, the Tennessee River substituted for the Mississippi River. "[Mooresville] is perfect for the setting of the 1845 story," explained the assistant art director, Keith Cunningham.

Jonathan and the other principal cast members arrived in Alabama in mid-April and immediately got to work. A typical day went something like this: All the actors and extras first reported to the wardrobe department between 6:00 A.M. and 8:00 A.M. The women wore period costumes from boots to bonnet. The men dressed in rugged frontier garb and carried muskets. Once they were dressed and had their makeup done, they waited until their scenes were called by assistant director Howard Ellis. After several rehearsals, he would determine if they were ready to shoot the scene for real—and then he would shout, "This is for the picture! Rolling! Action!"

One reporter who was on the scene was Deborah Storey of the *Huntsville Times*. Not only was she on the set writing articles for her newspaper, but she was also an extra and even had a scene with Jonathan! She was very impressed with his professionalism and wrote in one of her articles, "With extras, camera, and everything in place, Jonathan steps into position after pausing a moment to pat a horse that keeps sticking its nose into my back.... Jonathan is a real pro. He'll joke around until just the moment before he is to act, and then he is right on his mark."

Hitting his marks were old hat to Jonathan, but there was one part of the *Tom and Huck* shoot that was awkward for him: The Kiss! The on-screen smooch Tom Sawyer would share with Becky was a first for Jonathan. Before he even arrived on set, Jonathan was already answering questions about the possibility of a lip lock. He told *Teen Beat*, "How do I feel about it? It's *not* something I'd jump at the chance to do, but I guess if the script called for it, I guess I'd have to do it."

Of course, he knew that the script did indeed call for it, but Jonathan did not feel confident about it. But in the end, the kiss proved to be the least of Jonathan's worries. The set was plagued with bad weather, including hurricanes and tornadoes. That left everything wet, sticky, muddy, and full of mosquitoes. More than just an inconvenience, the weather put the shoot behind schedule by several weeks. That was one pressure. Another for Jonathan was finishing his schoolwork since the shoot overlapped his regular school year. Between scenes the kids were constantly being pulled into the schoolroom trailer so they could complete their required hours. Such close proximity, especially for Jonathan and Brad, could either build a bond or find the kids getting on each other's nerves.

JTT and Brad had very little in common. They came from vastly different backgrounds, family situations, and showbiz experience. Jonathan was his naturally talkative and friendly self, while Brad would go off by himself and play his guitar. Slowly, though, the boys began to talk—JTT was very interested in Brad's guitar playing and song writing. He was impressed by the poetry Brad wrote. Soon Jonathan's natural friendliness and good nature engulfed Brad. They warmed up to each other and a few weeks into filming could often be found joking around together. Their relationship was soon evident on-screen, and to the camera they weren't Jonathan and Brad but Tom and Huck!

On the other hand, Jonathan and Rachael's relationship didn't end up being as close, mainly because she didn't have as many scenes and was really only on the set at the beginning and the end of the shoot. She performed her scenes and then went home to return only as needed. However, when they did work together, Jonathan and Rachael clicked and helped each other through that awkward kissing scene, too.

Along with the bad weather, the very physical shoot, and school, the young stars had to squeeze in some set visits from the press, too. Though the producers tried to keep it to a minimum in order not to distract the actors, TV crews from CNN and *Entertainment Tonight* came down and taped segments. Reporters from major magazines and newspapers arrived with recorders and pencils in hand. Everyone wanted to get a look at and interview the "new" JTT. And though he was always polite and cooperative, what Jonathan really wanted to do when he wasn't working was to explore the neighboring towns and fish the streams. "There's a lot of bass fishing and there's some trout," he excitedly told *Teen Beat* before he left for *Tom and Huck*. "Alabama has a small coastline so you can go fishing at the coast. There's actually a lot of good fishing there."

Luckily, Jonathan *was* able to slip in a few fish days during the shoot, but by the end of June he was off and running to other things. Pretty soon the making of *Tom and Huck* was just a memory, though he was looking forward to attending the possible Huntsville premiere sometime in the winter of 1995. Until then, JTT wasn't going to slow down one bit!

THE FUTURE

In fourteen years JTT has achieved an amazing amount of success—indeed he has *already* left his mark on the world. But that doesn't mean he's about to sit back and rest on his laurels. Jonathan has a lot of plans, hopes, and dreams for the years to come.

Professionally, of course, he's returning for the fifth, sixth, and seventh seasons of *Home Improvement*. At the end of the fourth season, the cast and crew got together to celebrate their 100th episode. Jonathan hopes they'll be doing the same for number 200. But ever the realist, he knows to temper that dream with, "It's up to the fans how long we stay on the air."

While *Home Improvement* will always center around Tim Allen and his comedy, Jonathan will be meeting new challenges as Randy with each and every new episode. As Randy grows up, gets more involved with sports, school, and girls, Jonathan will be stretching his acting wings further and further. It's a prospect that excites him very much.

In fact, there'll be more JTT than ever to enjoy on *Home Improvement*. Fans can look forward to looking backward because in the fall of 1995, *Home Improvement* begins what's bound to be a long run in syndication—reruns forever! And, to launch this new chapter of the show, the producers have come up with a never-before-done "stunt"—they are actually taping a fresh episode of the show to kick off the syndicated season.

There has been some talk of a spin-off series from *Home Improvement* with Jonathan or even a totally new show starring the young actor, but if that happens, it's a long way off. As with all actors on the hit series, Jonathan's contract is for seven years. What will happen when the contract expires two years from now is anyone's guess, but there are those who believe that if Jonathan had to choose today, chances are he'd opt to drop out and go on to something entirely different Though he loves playing Randy, Jonathan always thirsts for the next challenge. It could be another TV series, but that's doubtful even though many have been offered. Truth is, now that he's gotten a taste of the big screen, he prefers the flexibility and challenge the movies offer.

Next up is another feature film, *Pinocchio*. The offer to star in this new movie came right on the heels of *Tom and Huck*. Indeed, the ink had barely dried on the *Tom and Huck* contract when *Pinocchio* poked his nose into the picture. Jonathan was thrilled to be able to say yes to this project because the timing was absolutely perfect. He had only a small window of opportunity between finishing *Tom and Huck* and returning to *Home Improvement,* and *Pinocchio* fit neatly into it. So after saying good-bye to his Alabama friends, he headed to England and then the city of Prague in the Czech Republic for three weeks of filming.

Pinocchio is an updated retelling of the classic children's fairy tale by Carlo Collodi about the puppet master Geppetto and his little wooden puppet, Pinocchio, who wishes to be a "real live boy." The puppet comes to life and goes on a trek to the legendary Terra Magico because only there will he find the way to become a "real" boy and truly be Geppetto's son. Along the way Pinocchio has many adventures, but he finally comes to realize that the magic was always in his heart, that love is what makes everyone "real." In this modern version of *Pinocchio,* Geppetto is a kindly computer scientist who makes a computer-generated boy, but the sentiments are still the same as in the legendary tale.

This new film will be a combination of animation, animatronics, and computer-generated imaging provided by the famous Jim Henson's Creature Shop. Of course, there will be live action sequences, as well. Jonathan will not only be the voice of the animated puppet—which was drawn in his very likeness—he'll also play Pinocchio when he becomes that "real" boy. Academy Award winner Martin Landau (*Ed Wood*) will be Geppetto.

An executive from Savoy Pictures, the company

that is releasing *Pinocchio,* told the *Hollywood Reporter,* "Martin and Jonathan are tremendous actors, and we are thrilled to have them create live-action roles for these fabled and timeless characters." No doubt, fans will be thrilled, too, when *Pinocchio* hits the theaters in the spring of 1996.

Naturally, Jonathan is always on the lookout for that next great script. "I really want to continue to do stuff that's different—just something that's a challenge every time," he insists. "I need to do something different to become a well-rounded actor."

Just *how* different does Jonathan want to go? Well, don't be surprised if he chooses something way off from his previous roles. He doesn't *always* want to play the good guy. In fact, he's already dreamed up the perfect breakaway role. Based on the movie *Silence of the Lambs,* which Jonathan admits was the scariest he's ever seen, he says he'd love to play the deranged villain, "a young Hannibal Lecter—imagine that character as a twelve-year-old kid. He'd probably already be nuts, but the voice would be soothing and manipulative. Now that would fun!"

Tom and Huck, Home Improvement, Pinocchio, and other movies—that's a lot, but not all that's upcoming for Jonathan. He's already posed for two posters that fans can buy, and several more are planned for release in the future. JTT has also completed the photographic work for a 1996 calendar—and word has it that there's another one in store for 1997!

Then there are Jonathan's long-range plans for the future. Though he loves acting, he also dreams of going *behind* the camera. In fact, some of JTT's idols are former kid actors who have made their mark as directors and producers. He cites Ron Howard and Jodie Foster as role models. "They survived what I call the child-actor syndrome and went on to become successful directors," he explained in an article in *USA Today*.

Why this career choice? Well, it's simple according to Jonathan. "Directing, I think, would be my ultimate goal," he told *New York Vue* magazine. "I find the behind-the-cameras aspect of the business more interesting. Don't get me wrong! I'm having a great time acting, but I think that after years and years, I'd get sick of it. In fifty years, I don't want to be asked, 'What have you done all your life'—and only be able to answer, 'I've been acting.' "

Pretty heady stuff for a fourteen-year-old, but Jonathan has always been taught he can do *anything* he sets his mind to, and he wants to try everything! "Show business is something I'm pretty familiar with," he told a reporter from the L.A. *Times*. "But I want to do it all—be an actor, write, direct—be a real Renaissance Man—yeah, that sounds good!"

On the personal side, Jonathan also has a multitude of plans. In line with his desire to try his hand at other aspects of showbiz, Jonathan is eager to develop all sides of his life and personality. And the first and foremost area is education. "Acting careers don't last a lifetime," he sagely announced in the L.A. *Times*, "so you ride it out and get the best education you can."

To that end, Jonathan looks forward to high school and then to college. There is no doubt he will go, no matter what. He loves learning too much to forgo it for anything.

"I'll go to college," JTT told *USA Today*. "I don't want my acting career to interfere with that, even if it's going really well. Henry Winkler went to Yale. So did Jodie Foster. And look where they are!"

And where might Jonathan pursue his higher education? Well, there's time to decide that, but he recently told an L.A. *Times* reporter he thought he'd investigate the Carnegie-Mellon (a university in Pittsburgh, Pennsylvania) business program.

Jonathan also plans to continue to work as hard and as often as he can on behalf of charitable causes. He was even able to fit in another Sail with the Stars cruise between *Tom and Huck* and *Pinocchio*. It was sponsored by the same people he sailed with in 1993, but this time the charity was the Tubular Sclerosis Foundation.

As for the *real* personal side of Jonathan's life, well, he hasn't had a real girlfriend yet, but that's very much on his mind and in his future. Eventually, one day, JTT sees himself married with children. And when he does find the girl of his dreams and makes that ultimate commitment, it will be forever. Love is not something Jonathan takes lightly, and he will only settle down when he knows it's right—and he will spend the rest of his life keeping it right!

What other dreams does Jonathan have? He wants to continue traveling all over the world. Now that he's seen a lot of the U.S. and been to Europe several times, he really wants to visit even more exotic places. He'd love to go fishing for black marlin in

Australia and visit New Zealand. And since *Home Improvement* is very popular in both Australia and New Zealand, a trip "down under" is not out of the question.

Jonathan also told *All-Stars* magazine, "I want to go to Africa. It has a lot of cool history to it. Even Asia and the Middle East. I'm looking forward to traveling all over the world."

In his travels, Jonathan hopes to find the perfect place to really put down *permanent* roots. Though right now Hollywood is where he has to be, JTT doesn't see himself there forever. "I read the out-of-state real estate ads," he told *Disney Adventures*. "I eventually want to move out of L.A. I wouldn't mind going back to the East Coast. I'm from Pennsylvania. [But] I don't know if I could take the winters."

What makes Jonathan determined to leave the town where he's found so much fame and fortune? Perhaps a peek in his bedroom at the poster on his wall answers that question. It's called the "Boulevard of Broken Dreams." Jonathan explains, "It pretty much represents Hollywood and all the great stars—Elvis, James Dean, Marilyn Monroe, Humphrey Bogart—who ended up sadly. It's a lesson that you don't want to end up that way. The title shows what it is—one day you're up there, having a good time, and the next, it all comes crumbling down all at once."

The fact is Jonathan wants to—needs to—keep everything in perspective. He's not about to let success go to his head and change who he really is. The "Boulevard of Broken Dreams" poster keeps that thought front and center for Jonathan. "That's one of the reasons I try to stay as normal as possible—it's important to stay a kid," he confided to an L.A. *Daily News* reporter. "You're constantly reminded of the horror stories around what I called 'child-actor syndrome.' But I have a lot of support."

Support, yes, from his family, friends, and his fans. But most importantly, Jonathan has inner strength from being a young teenager with a great big heart!

THE JONATHAN TAYLOR
THOMAS FACT FILE

Now that you've read Jonathan's entire story, here's a quick reference for all those 'JTT Facts at Your Fingertips' you need to know instantly.

Real Name: Jonathan Taylor Weiss

Why he uses a stage name: When he first became a professional actor, he found out that there already was someone with the same name in the Screen Actor's Guild. Since union rules state that you can't have two people with identical names registered with the Guild, JTT had to change his.

How he chose his stage name: Taylor is Jonathan's real middle name, and Thomas is his brother Joel's middle name.

Nickname: Is either JT, as Tim Allen calls him, or JTT, which the fan magazines have dubbed him. Family and friends just say Jonathan—no one calls him Jon or Jonny.

Birthday: September 8, 1981

Birthplace: Bethlehem, PA

Grew up in: Sacramento, CA and Los Angeles, CA

Hair & Eye Color: Blond, blue

Height, weight: 5', 80 lbs.—and growing every day.

Family: Mom is Claudine; dad is Stephen. Jonathan's brother Joel is 17.

Pets: Mac is the dog; Sami & Simba are the Himalayan cats—Sami is Simba's mom.

Lives now: In a split-level three-bedroom house in the San Fernando Valley section of Los Angeles.

In his room: Jonathan keeps his baseball and basketball card collections; sports trophies, fishing gear, and sentimental memorabilia. Posters of sports stars, ocean scenes, and the "Boulevard of Broken Dreams" cover his walls.

He collects: Autographs of his favorite sports stars

Favorites

Colors: Blue and turquoise

Actors: Robert De Niro, Anthony Hopkins, Jodie Foster, Glenn Close

Food: Vegetarian, pastas, artichokes, Caesar and Greek salads

Fruit: Honeydew and cantaloupe

Drink: Milk

Sports: Fly-fishing, roller hockey, tennis, baseball, basketball, football, boxing

Teams: Boston Celtics, New York Mets, Chicago Blackhawks, St. Louis Blues

Athletes: Michael Jordan, Larry Bird

Music: Boyz II Men, Shai, Silk, Billy Joel

Music he's not into: Alternative or rap

TV shows: Grace Under Fire, Roseanne, Fresh Prince of Bel Air, anything on C-SPAN and—ironically, since it's on opposite *Home Improvement—Frasier,* Also, sports events. "I watch a lot of sports," he tells, "especially anything on (the cable network) ESPN.

Movies: Forrest Gump, What's Eating Gilbert Grape, and "movies that keep you on the edge of your seat—that are never boring."

Places: New York and London

Magazines: Fishing magazines and *National Geographic*

Three things he likes more than acting: Fishing, soccer, hiking

THE JTT FACT FILE

Showbiz friends: Jenna von Oy: Carol Ann Plante

Person living or dead he'd most like to meet: Abraham Lincoln

People would be surprised to know: That like his TV dad, JTT is very interested in classic cars.

Secret: He's prone to migraine headaches.

Advice to young acting hopefuls: "You can't slack off in the acting business. You have to use all your energy in every role you try out for. If you don't, it will dampen your performance."

Worst problem in our country today: "AIDS. I just pray this whole thing will end soon. It's already plagued too many of our people."

The two most common questions he gets asked by fans (& His Answers)
Do You have a Girlfriend? "No."
How did you get the scar on your forehead? "I was high-sticked by accident during a roller hockey game."

Where to Write
You can send mail to JTT at any of these addresses:

c/o *Home Improvement,* ABC-TV, 2040 Avenue of the Stars, Los Angeles, CA 90067 c/o *Home Improvement,* Touchstone TV, 500 S. Buena Vista Street, Burbank, CA 91521

The Jonathan Taylor Thomas Fan Club, 18711 Tiffeni Drive, Suite 17-203, Twain Harte, CA 95383

If You Have a Computer and Are Online
Post your messages for Jonathan using America Online. Click on "Entertainment" in the main menu; then on ABC-TV Prime Time, and into *Home Improvement.*

Or, to trade messages with other JTT fans, click on America Online's Kids Only Bulletin Board.

Meet The Man!
Meet Shaq!

SHAQUILLE

O'NEAL A Biography

Shaquille O'Neal, the 7-foot-1 All-Star center for the Orlando Magic is dominating the world of big-time hoops with his size, quick smile and incredible basketball talent.

BILL GUTMAN

Available from Archway Paperbacks
Published by Pocket Books

1082-01

THE HARDY BOYS CASEFILES